SAVAGE CLAWS

NEW YORK PARANORMAL POLICE DEPARTMENT:
BOOK TWO

JOHN P. LOGSDON

BEN ZACKHEIM

Published by: Crimson Myth Press (www.CrimsonMyth.com)

Cover Art: Audrey Logsdon (www.AudreyLogsdon.com)

Thanks to TEAM ASS!

*Advanced **S**tory **S**quad*

This is the first line of readers of the series. Their job is to help us keep things in check and also to make sure we're not doing anything way off base in the various story locations!

(listed in alphabetical order by first name)

Bennah Phelps
Dana Arms Audette
Debbie Tily
Hal Bass
Ian Nick Tarry
Jan Gray
Janice Kelly
Jodie Stackowiak
John Debnam
Kevin Frost
Larry Diaz Tushman
Megan McBrien
Mike Helas
Natalie Fallon
Penny Campbell-Myhill
Rob Hill
Sandee Lloyd
Scott Reid
Sharon Harradine
Tehrene Hart

Thanks to Team DAMN

Demented And Magnificently Naughty

This crew is the second line of readers who get the final draft of the story, report any issues they find, and do their best to inflate our fragile egos.

(listed in alphabetical order by first name)

Adam Goldstein, Allen Stark, Amy Robertson, Anne Morando, Audrey Cienki, Barbara Henninger, Bonnie Dale Keck, Carol Evans, Carolyn Fielding, Chris Christman II, Cindy D., Darren Musson, Denise King, Dorothy MPG, Emma Porter, Helen Day, Ingrid Schijven, Jacky Oxley, Jim Stoltz, Jen Cooper, Julie Peckett, Kathleen Portig, Laura Cadger Rogers, Laura Stoddart, LeAnne Benson, Lindsay Stroven, Mary Letton, Melissa Parsons, Michelle Reopel, Myles Mary Cohen, Penny Noble, Pete Sandry, Sara Mason Branson, Scott Ackerman, Steve Widner, Susan Prentice, Terri Adkisson, Tony Dawson, Wendy Schindler, Zak Klepek.

CHAPTER 1

The cold froze my eyeballs.

I blinked away the sheets of ice and tossed my sandwich at the garbage can.

"Close the door, rookie!" Max yelled from the driver's side of his boat of a car.

The sandwich slid off the top of the pile of trash and plopped onto the sidewalk with a sick splat.

I slammed the car door shut and took in a deep breath of warm air.

After a moment of chattering teeth and rubbing my hands together, I felt my pixie partner's eyes on me and glanced over at him. His frown would have been kind of cute if it hadn't been attached to an asshole.

"What are you looking at?" I asked. "I closed the door, didn't I?" He kept glaring. "Look, Shakespeare. I know I can change into a tiger and I have magic claws and it looks like I can do just about anything, but I'm telling you for the last time, I don't read minds!"

"You gonna pick that sandwich up off the street, or what?"

I looked at the sandwich on the icy pavement and turned back to him. "The answer to that question is 'or what'."

"That's littering, Black," he said as he took a bite of his mini taco.

"It tasted like bile toast with fat-free mayo."

"PPD ain't allowed to litter. It's in our deal with the city. You break the deal, you break the trust. Got me?"

"Got you," I said, not moving.

"I'll have to report it," he said.

I had to change the subject or the lecture would go on for another hour. I wasn't going to go back out in that cold for anything. Tigers don't like cold.

"Doesn't this guy ever go anywhere?" I asked.

Max glanced up at the apartment window we'd been staring at for hours. It belonged to Micralp Proudass, a wizard with a messed up name who was a suspect in the kidnapping of my friend and fellow weretiger, Mike. We'd saved Mike from being experimented on the week prior, but one wizard escaped our raid.

The best lead we had was Proudass.

We were on our third shift in that stinky car and were sick and tired of even the thought of each other. Pixie farts sound like machine gun fire and smell like the sins of all of humanity given stench.

Max and I had been sniping at each other so much that we'd finally settled into a silence. The sandwich infraction was the first time I'd used my vocal cords in about eight hours.

Max leaned back in his booster seat. My plan to distract him seemed to be working. He sighed and said, "Wizards are fucked up. Proudass might never leave the apartment."

"If that's true, then I guess he's not our guy."

"You figure that out on yer own?"

"How does he eat? He's got to get groceries."

"Maybe he stockpiles food. Maybe he transports it in or some wizard shit like that."

My partner took a too-big bite and let taco meat dribble from his mouth.

"Maybe we could go undercover," I said. "Get someone to accidentally deliver Chinese food to him or something."

"Someone," Max parroted.

"Yeah, someone," I said back.

"You mean like a rookie?"

"Well, no, like someone who doesn't mind freezing his ass off out there."

"Sounds like a rookie to me."

"Maybe Graham. Or Fay."

"Go for it," Max said, shrugging. "You convince one of them bozos to do your dirty work for you, then more power to you. What? What are you looking at?"

"Nothing," I lied.

"No, you just looked at me like I stole your ball of yarn."

"Just—"

"Just what, Black?" His tone was getting dangerous. Max did not like to be kept in the dark.

"You're letting me do what I want," I said. "That's not normal."

He shrugged. "It's a good idea. We have to do something to get this guy to show us his routine, right?"

"Thanks, partner." I raised a hand up for a high five but he just frowned at it like it was goblin porn.

"Four more hours until we get our break," Max said. "Gonna grab some more coffee. Want some?"

"I'm good."

He opened the car door, sending a gust of ice air into my face, and flew out of the car and into the deli across the street. All of this happened in the time it took me to blink.

I rubbed my hands against my jacket and tucked them under my armpits. I wasn't sure how I'd handle the cold of a New York winter. I'd heard stories about it, but feeling it against my skin was a whole layer of pain I hadn't expected. I'd be a big girl about it, of course, but I'd bitch and complain on the inside.

Maybe Sir Pickle had something to keep me warm. The vampire ran the New York PPD armory so he had tech and spells coming out of his veins. I almost reached out to him on the connector, when I saw some movement in the apartment window.

It was the first sign of life we'd seen since day one. The wizard's back-lit silhouette reached for something and pulled down what looked like a book. It was hard to tell.

A shadow passed in front of the window.

I blinked and tried to adjust my eyes. I couldn't figure out what was going on for a second. I did a partial transform and my eyes sharpened.

It was a man.

Someone was standing outside the wizard's window. He was dressed in black. Crouched low.

I saw a flash of light from his hands, like a dagger glowing in the light of the street lamps.

The wizard was about to get some company.

CHAPTER 2

I threw the car door open. A wave of cold flowed into every hole in my face and made me choke. I coughed a couple of times before I was able to yell, "HEYRRRRR!"

It came out half-English, half-tiger.

But it did the trick.

The guy in the black outfit jerked and broke the window with his elbow. I heard Proudass scream.

I went full tiger.

And immediately regretted it.

The cold under my paws made my claws retreat instinctively and I fell nose-first into the hard sidewalk. I tried to shake it off but found myself wobbling toward the fire escape.

Proudass screamed again. This time he sounded like he feared for his life. My tiger ears knew that tone. My tiger nose knew that smell, too. The wave of stench carried on the wind told me he'd crapped his Merlin pajamas.

I calculated my leap onto the fire escape. I moved my head up and down slightly, and got a good read on the height. The surface was clear. Probably icy, so I got ready to compensate for that. I moved my back legs back an inch and grabbed the cement with my claws.

Ready.

"What the fuck are you doing?" Max shouted at me from the car.

I turned just in time to see his coffee slip off the roof and splatter all over the street. That should put him in a good mood after I saved the wizard.

But now I had to re-calculate the jump again. I growled a "goddammit" and started over.

"Black, get back here," Max yelled over the connector.

The voice in my head made me lose my concentration again.

I turned to my partner and roared, frustrated.

"Proudass is being attacked!" I yelled back via our connection.

I jumped high enough to reach the second level. My hope was that my claws could find a grip and get me the rest of the way up the fire escape. My back claws slipped on the ice. I barely grabbed the railing with my front paws. I hung there for a second before managing to pull myself up.

It wasn't pretty but it worked.

I raced up the zig-zagging ladder to the fifth floor. That's when I heard a struggle from inside the apartment. I transformed back to human form and pulled out my 6er, the special gun I'd received from Sir Pickle.

I slid to the edge of the window and tried to steal a quick peek inside.

There was a flash of light. I moved just in time to avoid getting hit by something. It passed right in front of my face, smacking into the bricks of the building across the street a split second later.

A knife.

Some jackoff had thrown a knife at me.

"That was a warning," a man's voice said from inside. It was a soft voice, calm. Scary calm.

"I have a warning for you too, creepy dude," I said. "Drop your weapons and step away from Proudass and I won't put this bullet in you."

I felt a flutter of wind near my head. I knew it was Max before he opened his mouth.

"What the fuck do you think yer doin', rookie?" my partner whispered in my ear.

He had his gun drawn.

"He's going to kill the wizard," I whispered back.

"So you just go run into the shit without letting me know?"

"There wasn't time. I tried to distract him."

"Yeah? How did that go?"

I knew where he was going with this string of thought. Once again, my decision didn't match his gut. And that meant he thought I'd just made things worse.

"I'll let you know in a minute." I turned back to the window. "Proudass! You okay?"

No answer. Maybe his attacker had a gun to his head. Maybe he was dead.

Max's wings fluttered faster and he hovered over the top of the window. He stopped his wings and twisted in the air, then started flapping them again. He was floating upside down. He slowly lowered himself from above and peeked through the window.

"No movement," he said via the connector. *"Dark. Can't see a thing."*

"Careful," I warned. *"He throws knives."*

"I throw bullets," Max replied as he zipped into the apartment, guns blazing.

Now there's one thing you should know about pixie guns. It took a lot of convincing to get pixies to handle guns at all. They liked to depend on their own traditional weapons to do their fighting. Dust, swords, spears, slingshots, that kind of thing. My 6er had been designed by a couple of pixies, but they were the exception. For every other officer of the pixie persuasion, the PPD had to customize the gun to make it acceptable to their picky dispositions.

For example, there were a number of pixies who preferred to have it so each bullet fired made a musical note.

Why? I had no idea at the time. I just knew that the spell to make musical ammo was a simple one and the PPD was happy to oblige if it meant an army of tiny, capable officers.

Max fired three shots.

Three notes.

C G G

Two knife-missiles zipped past my face. Two knives meant the perp's hands were empty. I had to act fast.

I dove into the apartment and rolled across a carpeted floor. It occurred to me as I came to a stop that the bad guy could have had an autoloader of some sort. Like an armband that held a bunch of throwing knives where he could throw one and have the next at the ready in a split second.

Another rookie mistake. Max would love to rub that in if we survived the night.

I sucked in some air as I realized my leg was cut by the window glass. I leaned on the back of a couch and applied some pressure to the wound.

Two more shots. Two more notes.

A G

Again, two more shots rang out. Or sang out, I guess.

I recognized the tune.

Everyone recognized the tune.

It was tough to stop yourself from finishing 'Shave and a Haircut' in your head.

I took a gamble.

If I was distracted by the song coming from the pixie gun then maybe our target was distracted too.

I partially transformed, so that my eyesight sharpened to tiger level.

Using the couch as cover, I aimed into the darkness. I spotted movement in the doorway of a room. Man-sized. It was either the knife thrower or the wizard.

"FREEZE!" Max and I yelled together.

B C

The final two bullets in his pistol were history.

Shave and a Haircut was complete.

A sick thump followed the end of the ditty.

I almost cried out to see if Max was okay, when I realized that the sick thump wasn't him hitting the ground. It wasn't the wizard or the dagger dickhead either.

It was me.

CHAPTER 3

First I felt the cold.

Like little daggers sapping my strength. Making my body shake so hard I lost control.

I sat up fast, sucking in some air and letting it out in a stream. I tried to see through the billowing mist of my breath.

"Settle down, kid," Max said. He stood next to me, his hands pressed hard on my side. "You got hit."

"You shot me?" I asked.

"No, I didn't shoot you, rookie," he said, offended. "You got a dagger in yer ass."

I looked down and saw a blade hilt poking out of my pants. Half the blade was dug deep into my thigh

"I'm not sure about pixie anatomy but that's not my ass, it's my thigh."

"Ass, thigh, it's all the same."

Max did that sometimes. He'd make zero sense and leave everyone around him looking at each other for clarification that never came.

"Where's the wizard?" I asked. "Is he okay?"

"Hell if I know. I saw you go down and covered you. Pretty sure the knife guy got away, though."

"We need to get that wizard, Max," I rasped, cringing as a slash of pain shot up my side. "Someone is trying to keep him quiet. He's our guy. He's got the claw."

"No shit?" he replied in a mocking way. He fluttered up into the air slightly while gripping his chest and giving me an incredibly dramatic look of awe. "I *never* would have guessed that! You think so?"

I rolled my eyes and leaned back against the couch. It hurt so damn bad.

My feet started to get cold.

"You think the blade could be poisoned?" I asked, wincing. "I can't feel my toes."

"Could be shock," Max said, landing again. "Just look at me and breathe, okay?"

"Yeah, sure," I said, but the second he suggested it could be shock, I started to get light-headed.

Suddenly, I felt trapped.

I couldn't have run if I wanted to.

"Heyheyhey, Black, stay with me," Max yelled, as he flew right up to my face and fanned me with his wings.

"Yeah, I'm good," I said but the words didn't sound right out of my mouth.

"Oh yeah, yer great! Half yer head is a tiger and the other is a pale rookie who wouldn't know how to follow an order if it bit her in the ass, thigh, or whatever."

"You're ordering me not to go into shock?" I managed to say as sparkles of light started to dance in front of my eyes, and a surging nausea bubbled up from my gut.

"What the fuck do you care? You never follow them anyway!"

He was really in my face now.

He shook his teeny finger in front of my nose and slapped its tip a few times.

Then he slapped me across the face.

So I barfed on him.

Hey, I didn't plan on it, but it did make me feel better right away.

He shook himself like a dog, vibrating most of the mess off of him and all over the wizard's floor.

"Sorry," I said, wiping my mouth.

"No, yer not," he griped as he rubbed up against a couch pillow. "You okay?"

"Yeah, yeah I'll be fine. Just, just find the wizard."

"Stay put," he said. "Don't move from that position. You think you can do that?"

I scowled at him, though it took a fair bit of effort. "Yes, I can do that!"

"Fine!" He flew off, muttering.

"Max!"

"What?"

"Thanks for slapping me," I groaned.

"My pleasure."

"I'm sure it was."

I took a deep breath and looked around the dark room.

"Hey, Sue," I said, using the connector to contact the NYPD's AI.

"What the fuck do you want?" he hissed. Sue's deep, male voice was heavy on the Brooklyn accent and light on the

empathy. Sue didn't like me.

"Could use an ambulance here," I said.

Even my head voice sounded quiet to me.

I was running on fumes. I hoped hard that Max wouldn't need my help anytime soon. I was in no shape to handle anything more than maybe a fae orgy.

"Why is you always telling me to do da things that Max just told me to do?" Sue asked.

"Because I'm new to this?"

"No shit! Maybe you should stay off the line until you catch up. In six years. Nice talking to ya!"

"Yeah, you too. Have a nice day." I then added, *"Note that I'm wiping your servers first chance I get."*

"Stand in line, rookie."

"Did Max ask for backup?" I asked before he could cut me off.

"No. Why?"

"Because the wizard is being attacked and some knife-throwing fucker might still be in the apartment with us."

"I'll send backup," Sue said.

That was surprising. He'd even lost the accent in his response.

"Great idea, Sue."

"Shit!" Max yelled from another room.

I gripped my 6er and used almost every bit of my strength to hold it up. I tried to move but the pain in my thigh slapped me down hard.

"Max!" I yelled. "You okay?"

"Fine!" he yelled back, and then grumbled something.

"You found the wizard?"

"Yeah," he said simply. "He broke up with his girlfriend."

"His girlfriend?"

"Yeah, Oxygen."

"Shit," I barked. *"Sue, we have a body here. Where's that backup, dammit?"*

He may have answered me. Maybe not. I only had the energy to focus on one thing at a time, and, at that moment, my focus was on the figure in the window.

It was the knife thrower.

He was backlit by the lamp outside. He shifted on his legs and something in his hands flashed bright enough to make me squint.

I lifted the 6er and got off a lame shot. It hit the radiator below the window. Only missed him by about five feet. So close.

He hopped through the window and bent over to pick something up.

The book.

The book I'd seen the wizard take off the shelf.

Dagger-dick slipped the book under his arm and crawled out of the window and onto the fire escape. He wasn't worried about me shooting him in the back. He knew I'd be lucky to get a shot off.

He turned to face me. The asswipe didn't move. He just stood there. I was at the mercy of a shadow.

I took a deep sniff. I wanted his scent. I wanted to know everything I could about my killer before he offed me. My tiger nose picked up on him and flooded my human brain with sensory information.

Max burst through a door, gun drawn.

I pointed my 6er in the general direction of the window and Max aimed his pistol.

But there was no one there.

The shadow was gone.

CHAPTER 4

"Is there a reason you gave me a heart attack just now, Black?" Max asked, his voice somewhat more calm than it probably should have been.

"He was on the fire escape," I muttered. "You must have scared him off."

Max zipped out the window. After a moment he floated back in. He twirled his gun on his finger and shoved it into the holster.

"I have that effect on the bad guys, yeah. No sign of him."

"You have that effect on the good guys, too," I chided him, fighting to stay awake.

"Yer giving me lip with a knife in yer ass?"

"Apparently." My breathing was a bit labored. "The wizard get stabbed, too?"

"Yeah, in the vitals, though. Not the way I want to go."

"Maybe Mike's claw is here," I said, swallowing hard before making a move to stand up.

I immediately dropped back to the floor.

"If it is, the bloods will find it," Max stated. "You just stay still and bleed like a good rookie."

"Bloods," I repeated. "Where have I heard of bloods?" I leaned my head back on the couch's armrest. "Wait. Are those the creepy bloodhounds?"

"Don't let them hear you call them that," Max said, taking a seat on the coffee table and looking around the living room.

"Creepy?"

"Bloodhounds. They aren't even dogs but they sure look like dogs. Sound like dogs, too."

Max carefully unwrapped my fingers from my pistol and slid the gun away from me.

Wise.

"Who the hell was that assassin?" I asked. "We know anyone who prefers daggers?"

Max hovered in place for a second, staring right at me. His expression was unreadable.

He flew toward me so fast that I thought he was going to slap me again. But instead, he landed near my leg and leaned toward the hilt of the blade still sticking out of my ass…erm thigh. Whatever.

A second later, he flew off in total silence. I knew him well enough to know he was talking to someone on the connector. But whatever he was saying, he was keeping it from me.

"Hey," I said. Max floated back to me and took another look at the dagger's hilt, ignoring me. "Hey!" I repeated.

"Quiet, kid," Max said. I wanted to strangle him, but I didn't think that would go over well with HQ. I mean, I'd probably gain a few fans if I took Max out, but…

After a minute of watching him swing back and forth across the room, mumbling, I cleared my throat. Max glanced up at me as if he'd forgotten I was there.

"Listen to me, Black, and listen close," his little eyes looked serious. "We got a problem here."

"What's going on, partner?" It was almost as if I'd had too much to drink. "Care to share?"

"You telling me that the guy you saw enter this apartment earlier is the same guy you just saw in the window now?"

"That's what I'm saying, yeah."

"You sure you didn't hallucinate him?"

"I just barfed all over you in shock so, no, I can't be sure." I giggled a bit. "I'm a bit out of sorts. I may also be buzzing a bit."

"Okay, stay still," he said. "This may hurt." He put both hands on the knife's hilt and in one swift movement he yanked it out.

The stars came back.

I was swimming in a dark cloud of flashing images. When my vision stabilized, I saw Max next to me. He sat cross-legged, applying pressure to my wound with one hand and staring at the dagger in his other.

"What the hell did you do that for, Shakespeare?"

He didn't answer me. I didn't have the patience or the energy to ask again. I let my head lean back and hoped for sleep. That would make the pain go far away.

"We've got trouble, kid," Max said, right as I was fading into sweet darkness.

"Hmmm?" I managed to say.

"The dagger," he said.

He held it up. The sharp tip gleamed in the street light. Just below the tip was a mark of some kind. I couldn't make it out at first. I formed my tiger eyes and saw that it was a capital H.

"H? What's H for?"

"Hunter," Max said. His tone was a couple of octaves higher than usual, and his voice cracked. I didn't like that at all. "We're up against The Hunter."

CHAPTER 5

That's when Sue decided it would be a good time to pipe in.

"EMTs are in the building. Bloods are en route."

"Thanks, Sue," Max replied, staring at the knife.

"You got it, bruddah," Sue quipped.

It seemed that Max and Sue got along famously. That figured.

"Who's Hunter?" I asked.

"*The* Hunter," he corrected me. "Assassin, like you said. He has a rep, though. Always gets his target."

"Is he a werewolf?" Most assassins are werewolves, which makes sense. Super strength, stealth when they want it, change shape while on the run. "Didn't smell like one, but I don't know what the hell I was smelling, especially with my head swimming."

Max shrugged. "No one knows what the hell he is. But I can tell you one thing. He's dangerous. And he's the last little shit I want to go up against with everything going on."

The apartment door smashed open, flying off its hinges. The wood frame splintered into a thousand pieces. When the mess settled, a large man stood in the doorway. He filled up the whole thing, height and width.

"Goddammit, Dick!" Max yelled.

"WHATTA WE GOT?" the man hollered.

He stepped into the dim light and crushed pieces of door under his shit-kicker boots. They were laced up to his knee. His pants were tucked in, giving him a Canadian Mounty look that matched his ridiculous fifty gallon hat.

"We got an officer down, you lead-licking, too-dumb-to-breathe, evolutionary-afterthought," Max screamed.

"ASS WOUND!" Dick yelled, and he dove with all the grace of a tripping bull.

He rolled toward us, stopping just short of slamming into me before he pushed himself up into a kneeling position.

"It's not my ass," I shot back. "That is the thigh. See? The thigh!"

Dick and Max looked at the red gash in my pants. Then they looked at each other and said, "Ass" at the same time. Except Dick yelled it loudly.

Max slapped Dick on the back of the head. "And now she has splinters in her face thanks to yer 22-IQ entrance there!"

"SORRY, BOSS!"

"Don't call me boss!"

"OKAY, BOSS!"

"Why is he yelling?" I asked.

"That's his normal voice," my partner replied. "He doesn't have the brain cells to control his volume."

"HE SAYS I USE EVERY OUNCE OF STRENGTH TO KEEP MY HEART BEATIN'," Dick said, and punctuated it with a belly laugh that made one of the cheap ceramic pieces in the apartment crack.

I gestured for Max to come close as Dick knelt next to me and opened his medic bag. Max just stared back at me, clueless. I gestured to him harder and showed him my gritted teeth.

"I THINK SHE WANTS TO TALK TO YOU, BOSS!"

Max sighed and got closer. I grabbed him and put him on the armrest next to me. Dick was focused on his bag as I whispered in Max's ear. "Should this guy be working on me?"

But Max didn't have time to answer. Dick tore half my pants off in one quick move.

"OOOOOOOOEEEEEEEEE!" he yelled, making me squint in pain. "THAT IS ONE NASTY KNIFE WOUND!"

"No, he shouldn't be working on anyone," Max said.

"Dick," a woman's voice hollered from the apartment door, "I told you to wait for me!"

I could just peek past Dick's wide shoulder to see a small woman, about five feet tall, standing with her hands on her hips. Hips that were covered in a massive belt that was packed with medical supplies.

"SORRY, PAT," Dick said as he swabbed some ointment of some kind on my wound. I hissed in pain. "SORRY, OFFICER BLACK,"

"Yeah, you're always sorry, Dick," Pat grumbled as she climbed over her partner's mess, pulling a gurney with her. "But you keep doing the same crap over and over again. I wonder why that is?"

"He's dumb as a Joe-Bob Chilling Trout?" Max asked.

Pat turned to him as if she just noticed he was there.

"It's one of those mechanical singing fish on the wall," Max explained.

"No, I think it's because he thinks he knows better," Pat stewed. "Dick got a promotion, and I think he's letting it get to his head." She peeked over Dick's shoulder. "Good job. Now, get her on the gurney, Dick."

"YOU GOT IT, PAT."

He lifted me up gently and laid me down like I was a baby. Pat strapped me in as Dick checked his work on my leg.

"I don't need to go yet," I said. "I want to meet the bloods."

Dick and Pat looked at each other before they both started laughing.

"What's so funny?" I asked Max when it was clear that the EMTs weren't going to come up for air anytime soon.

"No one has ever said that," Max said, shaking his head. "Kid, you do not want to meet the bloods."

"Yeah, I d…." But I didn't get a chance to finish my sentence as Dick wheeled me into the hallway and to the elevator before I could blink.

Dick filled my field of vision. His big smile was part-weird and part-comforting. I had to admit, he'd done a good job on my leg. The stinging had died down and it felt supported in the splint.

I was about to thank him for his work when he broke into song.

"ROCKABYE BAAAAABY ON THE TREETOP!"

I looked at Pat, hoping she could stop him, but she just shrugged.

"I'll see you in the infirmary, kid," Max said via the connector. *"We've got a lot of work to do. This case just got a hell of a lot more complicated. You got a day to get better. That's an order."*

CHAPTER 6

The infirmary was just down the hall from the main room of PPD HQ. Its high ceilings were covered in waves of lifeless LED lamps that cast an even sheen over everything, making the world look two-dimensional.

The room must have been sound-proofed because I couldn't hear a thing. I was alone, letting the medicine and spell do its work, passing time with only the thoughts in my head to keep me company.

Thoughts about the Blood Claw.

The wizards had come this close to using Mike's claw to make an army of mobgoblins with the abilities of a tiger. We caught most of the wizards, but the one that got away with the claw had made the mission a failure. At least in my eyes.

Max was more patient about it. Probably because of his veteran, seen-everything perspective. But I didn't have that perspective. Not at all. The case left me feeling incomplete. It felt like a dangling thread just hanging there, taunting me. It ate at me until I wanted to eat it back.

I growled.

That was the second time I'd partially transformed into a tiger without knowing it in the last week. I needed to get a hold of my emotions.

Keep the pride in check.

"Pride will kill you," as the old weretiger saying goes. Smart saying. The old, infamous tiger pride had taken our numbers down to two. If I didn't keep a lid on it, Mike would be carrying the weretiger mantle all on his own.

"There you is," Bob said as he smacked the door out of his way.

His cousin, Lou, followed right behind. His face lit up when our eyes met.

Bob and Lou. My goblin body guards. Former mobgoblins.

Yeah, I was the only PPD officer with bodyguards. Laugh it up, if you want, but the two of them had come in handy on our previous mission. We'd only saved Mike because they'd set us up with their bonkers granny. She'd pointed us in the right direction and the rest is history.

Bob marched right up to my bedside and gave me a look like he wanted to thrash me.

Lou stepped in front of him, all smiles.

"How the hell are ya, girl?" Lou asked.

"Like hell. You?"

"Reamed up the butt by the boss," Bob growled.

"What he means to say is, we've been better," Lou

clarified, trying to keep the smile on his face, but not doing a good job.

"Why does your butt feel reamed, Bob?" I asked with as much patience as I could muster.

It wasn't my fault their boss was such a jerk. And it wasn't my decision to have them tail me everywhere I went.

"Our asses hurt after the whoopin' the Director gave us for letting you go on this stakeout without us!"

"We're going to…" Lou started to say.

His eyes met mine and he murmured the rest of the sentence.

"Going to what?" I asked. When he gave me the puppy dog eyes, I lowered my voice. "Going to what, Lou?"

"We're gonna be on yer tail 24-7," Lou said. "Director's orders."

"The Director is right, though," Bob said, pointing his finger at me like a scolding school teacher. "It's one thing to spend a few hours watching a wizard. But three days? What if he'd been dangerous? He could have taken you out and you wouldn't know what hit you."

"That's my job, Bob," I replied. "The wizard sat on his ass for the whole time. Not a peep on the phone, the connector, the internet. No shopping for food. Nothing."

"We heard he bit the rocket," Lou said.

"The bullet," Bob corrected.

"The what?"

"The bullet! He bit the bullet!"

"Why the hell would he bite a bullet?"

"Why the hell would he bite a missile?"

"It's a saying. You know, like, how the hell could anyone ever bite a missile? It's ridiculous and that's the point!"

"So's biting the bullet!"

"Guys, please, keep it down," I complained. They kept frowning at each other. "Besides, he bit the knife."

"He got stabbed? Who stabbed him?"

"Some assassin who likes to use knives."

Bob and Lou stopped frowning. Bob wiped his face with his hand like he'd heard about the end of the world.

"The Hunter?" Lou asked me.

"That's the thought," I answered. "There was an H on the blade. Near the tip."

Bob and Lou weren't psychic, at least as far as I knew, but I'd swear they were communicating silently. Their eyes locked and their lips pursed.

"Okay, that's enough of that," I said. "You two look like you're synchronizing stomach pangs. Tell me what you know about this guy."

"He kills people," Bob muttered.

"Oh, really? I'm glad you told me that. I wouldn't have guessed." I dropped my sarcasm. "Now tell me something useful, please. Come on, guys."

"He's been around for a long time," Lou added. I knew he'd be more helpful than Bob, but I couldn't trust everything out of his mouth. His primary job was to protect me, so if he thought a piece of information could lead to danger, he'd suppress it without a second thought. "And he never misses."

"He missed me," I said. "I mean he hit me in the thigh, but he didn't kill me."

Bob and Lou glanced at each other. It felt like they were hiding something.

Bob shrugged and broke the silence by changing the subject. "I thought he was dead," he said, as if that answered my question.

"Why did you think that?" Max asked as he flew into my room.

"How long you been listening, pixie?" Bob growled.

"Answering a question with a question is rude," Max growled back. "Yer momma never taught you that?"

My partner lit up a cigar, never breaking eye contact with Bob.

"Max," I said, with a small cough. "I don't think you're allowed to—"

"I thought he was dead because he stopped killing, genius," Bob broke in.

"Yeah?" Max replied with a squint. "Killers take a break sometimes? I think yer lyin' to me, goblin. I think you know something about The Hunter that we don't."

Bob pulled himself up onto my bed and took a seat next to my feet. "There's a lot I know that you don't, cop."

"Hunter's never killed a wizard before," Max said, landing on the pillow next to my head. He smelled like a smokestack. "Any idea why he'd take a risk like that?"

Bob stuck his thumb in his own face. "What, you think I'm the jerk's best friend or something?"

"I'm just sayin', you hid a lot from us on the Blood Claw mission. I had to figure out how helpful you could be and then my partner here had to beg like one of those big-eyed kittens for you to throw us a bone."

I couldn't disagree. I mean, Max *was* being unfair to

my bodyguard buddy. No doubt about it. Just because Bob and Lou had secrets didn't mean they knew everything about every dirty deed in the city. Still, there was something about the way Bob was acting that made me wonder if Max was right. Bob couldn't look me in the eye. His body language was defensive.

Bob was backing down. Bob never backed down until you had him in a death grip.

"Bah," Max grunted. "Tired of getting water from this stone. Keep yer secrets. I'll find out in good time, and then we'll see how tough I gotta be on you two kitten tails."

Uh-oh.

"Who you callin' Kitten Tails?" Lou asked.

It was tough to get Lou angry, but Max was doing a great job. He'd been coming up with nicknames ever since he'd met Bob and Lou. None of them stuck. At least not until that moment. I could tell from the smirk on Max's face that Kitten Tails was my partner's new, official name for the goblin team.

It was my turn to change the subject. "Guys, if he never misses then why am I still alive?"

Bob and Lou glared at Max who took a big puff of his cigar and let it out with a smirk on his face.

"Because he wasn't hired to kill you, BB," Lou said just before he stormed out.

Bob picked up his jacket from the chair and looked at me. "Yeah, if you're not the target, you have a chance in hell of seeing the dawn. See you soon, sweetheart."

"See you, Bob."

Bob nodded his head at Max. "Asshole," he hissed.

Max watched him leave.

"You have a way with people, Max," I said as he blew out a tiny smoke ring. "Maybe you should lay off a little. They're going to be with us everywhere we go."

"I can handle 'em."

"It's not you I'm worried about."

CHAPTER 7

My bedroom was one of the small offices on the perimeter of HQ's Main Room.

Yeah, it sucked.

When I was released from The Zoo, I got dropped into the tiny space. I thought it was going to be temporary, but I was beginning to get the sense that moving me somewhere more private was not a top PPD priority.

They may have released me from the infirmary, but I could still feel the eyes on my door. If I took a step into the Main Room I was immediately tracked by whoever was on Bethany duty. It wasn't like the officers hid it from me. And Sue, the AI, loved to be the one to tell me to hurry it up in the bathroom. Such a dick. I was more determined than ever to find the AI servers and see what kind of damage my tiger claws could do to them.

Servers.

That reminded me. I needed to talk to Pickle. Sir Pickle was the tech genius around the NYC PPD. He hung out in a dark wing of HQ and concocted tech magic, and real magic, too. I didn't know him that well, but, then again, no one did. He was a recluse.

Still, he'd been around a while. He knew a lot. I could ask him about The Hunter and he might even fill me in on the Blood Claw ritual. I'd been poking around for info about the mysterious spell that could endow anyone with the abilities of a tiger, but I'd found zip. My friend and fellow officer, Fay, was trying to extract some details from her mother, a powerful witch by her own telling. But so far, nothing.

I recognized the sharp knock on my door.

"Come in, Fay," I said.

She poked her head in. "How did you know it was me?"

"You always do something rhythmic."

"Shave and a haircut..."

"Two bits." That reminded me of the tune that Max's pistol had made in the wizard's apartment. Weird how things like that can pop up in our lives multiple times, like some kind of cosmic pattern. Heavy. "Any word from your mom about Blood Claw?"

"That's why I'm here."

Fay sat down on the end of my bed and I placed my book down on the side table, excited. I sat up straight and leaned forward.

"The spell originated from the weretiger elders, actually."

"Wait, what? Why would weretigers make a spell that used their own claws to give the power of the tiger to anyone? That makes no sense."

"My mother told me it was the result of the weretiger

population dying out. They wanted to find a way to continue their species."

"But I thought it only gave someone the ability to run fast and smell well and all of that. Not to transform into a weretiger."

"That is all it does, but the elders who crafted the magic died off before they could perfect it. If they'd been given more time they could have saved your species."

"Instead, they created an easily-weaponized potion that any two-bit crook could steal and use for his own purposes."

Fay didn't say anything, but her silence told me she agreed.

"Don't tell me," I added. "The elders didn't look for guidance from other supers or scientists, did they?"

Fay nodded. I sighed and buried my head in my hands. It was just a lot to take in. Even when facing our own demise we didn't listen to our own advice.

"Pride will kill you," Fay said, breaking the heavy silence.

"How did you know about that?"

"I read, Beth," she said, frowning.

"We're just such morons, Fay. When will weretigers learn?"

I didn't expect her to answer, but she said. "I guess it's up to you."

I smiled at her and shrugged.

"We're doomed then," I admitted.

"If Mike is as dense as you say he is, then maybe."

She was trying to be funny, but it struck a little close to home. Mike was a dear friend. He was like a brother.

But he always made bad choices. Selfish choices. He was even holding back on sharing his little swimming boys with scientists who could possibly save our species. He said he was holding out for a good price.

"What else is needed besides the claw for the ritual?" I asked.

"Five wizards. But Mom wouldn't tell me any more than that. She probably thinks I want to try it out. She doesn't trust me."

"Sorry, Fay. I didn't realize that when I asked you to do some digging."

"It doesn't matter. Mom can't get to me anymore. I'm a PPD officer now, so she can just suck it."

"Okay," I said, smirking. Fay wasn't exactly a foul-mouthed faerie. So hearing her let loose like that was, well, hilarious. I barely stopped myself from laughing. "You want to take a walk with me?"

"Sure! If the doc says it's okay."

"Yeah, I'm back on duty later today. She told me to get the blood flowing again."

"That's a weird choice of words, all things considered."

"Doc isn't known for her tact."

It wasn't exactly fun, but I made my way out of my room and cut left, doing my best to look like I wasn't in any pain at all.

"Where are we walking?" asked Fay.

"To the lab."

Her smile faded. Fast.

"The Sauerkraut guy?"

"Sir Pickle, you mean. Yeah. Why?"

"I just remembered that I have to do… something."

She scurried off, weaving between the desks like they were an obstacle course. Within seconds, she was completely out of eyesight.

"That was weird," I said out loud.

"Not as weird as you naked," Sue said over the intercom so everyone could hear.

"Finding the servers now, asswipe!" I yelled back as I made a straight line for the lab doors.

CHAPTER 8

"Sir Pickle?" I called out into the pitch dark.

No answer.

I flicked on my pen light, standard PPD gear. I flashed it over the walls. They were lined with shelves, packed to the hilt with so much stuff that I couldn't make out anything. It may as well have been a collection of garbage, as far as my eyes were concerned.

I spotted a shiny box.

It was a cross between a treasure chest and a toaster. It's bright sheen glittered in the penlight while its iron latch was dark as a moonless night. I flicked the latch with my fingernail. It didn't open. I glanced around to make sure Pickle wasn't standing right behind me. I pulled harder on the latch until it popped open.

A low rumble shook the whole room.

"Containers don't always contain," the voice said from somewhere in the room. "Do you know why, Officer Black?"

I closed my eyes.

Busted. That was Pickle's voice.

"Because curious busybodies open them when they shouldn't?"

"I like you, Bethany Black," he said in a cool voice, "but do not touch anything in my lab. It is for your own safety. Curiosity killed the cat, remember?"

"Sorry, Sir Pickle," I replied, though I wanted to give him shit about the cat-comment. I glanced back at the box. "It's like it beckoned to me."

"It did," he said, appearing out of the silky black and looming over me. I thought vampires didn't float, but I would have bet my badge that he was walking on air. "And it hoped to be contained no longer."

"What is it?"

"In the box? It's the tide of blood through your veins, and the toil of a thousand souls. It's the intent of a dying madman and the spark of death in a newborn."

"Sounds like it would be fun at a party," I said.

"It depends on the party, I suppose."

"I was joking," I mumbled.

"Hmmm. Funny." He didn't look amused, but I don't think that smooth white face had broken a smile of consequence since leeches were all the rage. "I, however, was not joking. What can I do for you, Bethany Black?"

"I need information."

"That is something which I have in abundance," he replied in a grandiose way. "Launch the query across the infinite space of halves between us."

I just looked at him.

"Shoot," he clarified.

"Ah, okay, sorry. So I don't know if you've heard about

the mess I got into with Max." It was a leading statement. He just stared down at me, not taking the bait. "Yeah, so, anyway, it looks like we may have run into an obstacle in our case."

"What kind of obstacle?"

"One called The Hunter. Heard of him?"

His expression didn't change. No surprise there. But the pause he took was as pregnant as a bunny in a bunny club on Bunny Ecstasy.

"Yes," he said, simply.

He probably would have left it at that if I didn't follow up.

So I followed up.

"Can you tell me what you know?"

"I know he kills without mercy," he answered without inflection. "I know he appears to enjoy his work. I know he kills for hire. I know he leaves no clues, no patterns, nothing for our best officers to follow."

Clearly, he knew a lot of the same stuff we already knew. I had the feeling there was more to this onion than the top layer, though.

"When did he last kill someone?" I asked, not sure if he knew or not.

"Before I started here," he answered with a sigh. "I've wondered when we'd face his chaos again. You were at the crime scene, correct?"

"Yeah, he tossed a dagger in my thigh."

"Hmmm."

"Hmmm, what?"

He raised a judgmental eyebrow. "I'd heard it was not your thigh that felt the dagger's plunge."

"It was my thigh, dammit."

"Whatever you say, Bethany Black." I took in a deep breath and let it slowly escape. "I did not know it was The Hunter that you were up against. You are fortunate to breathe the air of this life and not the one that comes moments before entering the Vortex."

"Yeah, that's what I gathered. That blade was sharp as hell."

"Do you have it?" he asked. There was an edge to the question, as if he'd been meaning to ask it of me from the moment I walked into his lab.

I glanced at him sideways.

"*I* don't," I replied, "but evidence does."

He let out a crackling sound. Something between a cough and a sigh. A laugh, maybe?

"I certainly doubt that."

"Yeah? Why? That's standard OP."

"Not when it comes to The Hunter, Bethany Black. His evidence disappears as fast as it comes in. I've tracked his crimes for years, even as an amateur sleuth, and his blades disappear as quickly as they kill."

It dawned on me that Sir Pickle had quite a history. I made a silent vow that I would find out more about him, if time ever allowed for it.

"Well, why don't you ask evidence for it and see what happens?"

He looked down on me, eyelids at half mast.

"Done," he said, having just used the connector to make the request. "But I assure you that—"

He was cut off by the whooshing sound of the blade being delivered in the transfer tube.

His eyes went wide in the closest approximation of surprise I'd probably ever see on his face.

I slid the tube's door open and pulled out the dagger that had been in my thigh only the day before. It was bagged up and marked.

He took it from my hand as if it were an ancient relic. His demeanor suggested he had to be careful or the blade may distintegrate into dust. Like a man who was holding the most volatile explosive substance in the world, he laid it on a steel slab and pulled it from the plastic.

"Shouldn't you wear gloves?" I asked.

"I'm a vampire, Officer Black," he replied without taking his eyes off the knife. "I don't have oil on my skin."

"Oh yeah," I breathed. Idiot. Rookie question. "I forgot."

He was silent as he looked at the blade closely. He held it up and examined the tip with one eye as he kept the other one shut.

"Fascinating."

Sir Pickle moved to a lab table with a microscope on it. He slid the blade onto the platform and leaned over to get a better look.

After a few seconds he stood up straight, turned to face me and took a seat on the lab table.

"Are you okay?" I asked. He turned as white as a ghost, which is packed with irony being that he was a vampire. "Sir Pickle?"

"Fine," he rasped. Then he cleared his throat and blinked a few times. "Yes, I'm fine."

"What's wrong? Did you find something?"

"I found out what the blade is made of. It's a rare

polymer. Known only to a select few supers and *no* normals. Its lightness and strength are a dream to most, an aspiration that no mortal ever expects to achieve."

"But *you* know about it?"

"Know about it?" he asked as he looked up at me with wide eyes. "I invented it."

CHAPTER 9

I knew Sir Pickle had secrets, but, at that moment, I realized I had a lot to learn about our resident vampire genius.

"You look as if the Romans just lost the Battle of Metaurus," Pickle noted.

"If that means I look like I'm surprised, then yeah, I guess I am."

"I've pumped the blood of innovation through a number of advancements over the years," he explained. "As both leader and follower."

"Yeah? Who have you worked with?"

He studied me for a moment. I met his stare and tried not to blink. I'd stepped into a staring contest. A tiger vs. vampire staring contest. Was this a test of some kind? If it was, he was about to meet his match. Cats can stare forever.

But I didn't realize that vampires could, too.

I'm not sure how long we stood there, but by the time there was a knock on the lab door, we were in the thick of, well, whatever we were in the thick of. Pickle didn't blink. Neither did I.

A bright light from the Main Room flooded the space for a moment as the door slid open.

"You in here, Bethany?" Graham called out.

Officer Graham was deaf, so I usually responded to him with the connector in situations where he was looking for me. Not this time, though.

If Pickle was going to stay silent, then so was I.

The lab door slid shut and Graham's flashlight beam darted around the long, thin room until it settled on us.

We must have been quite a sight.

"There you are," Graham said. "Why didn't you answer me just now?"

He aimed his light in my face to read my lips.

I didn't blink.

Pickle's eyebrow arched, impressed with my staring skills.

"Hello?" Graham asked. He waved his hand in between our faces. "What the hell are you two doing?"

Pickle and I didn't say anything.

I was following his lead.

I was determined to do what he did. If this was a test that would help him trust me, then I was going to pass—or dry my eyes out trying.

"Okay, you two are freaking me out more than you usually freak me out, so can you just cut the bull and answer me, please?"

Sorry, Graham.

"Shit," Graham said. "Looks like a spell of some kind." He started to pace. "What do I do? What do I do?"

He was thinking out loud.

I felt bad, but it was more important that I keep up with the vampire than spare Graham any embarrassment.

"I could call in Max," he stated. "No, he'd just ride me about how I always need him to help. Asshole."

He waved his hand in front of our faces again.

"Okay, they're breathing, at least. That's good. Let's see. I could turn. But what if I turn into a honey badger again?"

Graham was a werewhatever. He could change into a bunch of different animals, which was cool, except he had zero control over what animal he'd become. He could be something harmless or something dangerous. Something he could control easily, or something that could take him over.

"BOO!" he yelled at both of us.

It was a good move.

I jumped on the inside. But I didn't blink.

Neither did Sir Pickle.

Yeah, the whole thing was stupid. But my tiger pride had kicked in. I wasn't going to lose this contest. I'm not sure why the stakes felt so high, but they did.

The lab door slid open and the noise of the Main Room flooded the darkness along with the light.

"Oh, fer cryin' out loud," Max barked.

"They're under some kind of spell," Graham said, waving at him to keep his cool.

"Yeah, they are," Max said as he flew up to me and entered my field of vision. "The Stupid Moron Spell. Its effect can be felt across all rookies who think they have free rein over the PPD and can stick their noses into the deep, dark corners whenever they want." My partner turned to Sir Pickle and put his finger in his face. "Stay away from the new meat, vampire. Got me?"

At first I didn't think Sir Pickle would budge, but then his eyes shifted ever so slightly and settled on Max.

In one swift move, Pickle retreated into the dark corner of the lab and appeared to…disappear.

"Creepy jerk." Max turned to me and shivered. "Black, suit up. Briefing room in two minutes."

"What's going on?"

"If the buzz is right, we've got another dead wizard."

CHAPTER 10

I wasn't at 100%, but I wasn't going to remind anyone of that. We gathered in the briefing room, a long and thin mini-theater. Sarge waited at the podium for all of us to file in.

"No, no, take yer time, people," he jibed with a healthy dose of sarcasm. "Don't rush on my account."

We never moved fast enough for Sarge.

"Metropolitan Museum," he stated, finally. "One wizard down. We have two officers on the scene. Sue picked up on the supernatural activity before any of the normals, but we have to move fast to lock the place down and get the clues we can get."

"How was he killed?" I asked.

He pursed his lips and shot me with a glare that made my stomach clench. "You wanna wait for the next sentence before you go askin' questions, Black?"

"Sorry, sir."

"Yeah, you say that a lot." He held his gaze on me for another couple of seconds. "Cause of death was guts all over the fuckin' marble floor. Reason for said spectacle is undetermined at this time, but you and Shakespeare get to go and find us some answers."

"We're on our way, boss," Max said.

"Hold off, Max," Sarge commanded. "Got a message from under foot that the goblins are goin' with you."

"Screw that!" Max yelled. He hated it when Bob and Lou tagged along. "Tell them they can stick their orders where the moon don't shine, Sarge."

"You think I didn't?" Sarge shot back. "City Hall wants it, too, Max. That means we're gonna deal with it. Black's former warden is makin' a stink that lingers, I guess. Mayor wants her off his back, stat." He sneered at me. "So we get to bend over and smile."

"What else is new?" Max mumbled.

"World's smallest violin," Sarge said, rubbing his fingers together.

"Is that what you call it?" Max countered, clearly incensed. "I thought its name was 'LargeSarge'."

The whole room made a noise that was a cross between a foghorn and a tire losing all its air.

Sarge pointed his finger at Max for a good ten seconds before he managed to get his voice to work.

"With that kinda attitude," he growled, "I think you get Franklin and Graham, too, asshole."

I shot my partner a look and he met my eyes. He swallowed his comeback.

"Wait," Fay said. "Why do we have to be punished?"

"Zip it, Franklin," Sarge grumbled. "If that's all the insubordination for the day, I got one more point of order." He held up a piece of paper. "We've had a number of small break-in reports from museums around the city. Small stuff. Broom closets. Employee bathrooms. May be related to this case, may not. But keep yer eyes and ears and noses open. Dismissed."

I chased after Max as he walked down the stairs to the garage.

"What's wrong with you?" I asked Max as we walked into the garage. Fay and Graham walked ahead of us.

"Whatta ya mean?" he growled, ready for battle, as usual.

"Talking back to Sarge like that. It's not like you."

"What the hell do you know about me, exactly, Black? Huh?"

I gave him a look. "I know that you usually don't bark at Sarge like you bark at the rest of us."

"Yeah?" He adjusted his hat a few times and double-checked the buttons on his overcoat. "You figure that out after a whole month on the force?" He started pointing at me as he continued gliding toward our ride. "Lemme tell ya somethin'. I treat him like shit all the time, okay?"

"Oh, my mistake," I said, adding a little too much drama to my you're-full-of-shit-Max body language.

"You know what?" he blurted, flying quickly in front of me while holding up his middle finger. "Screw this. Yer not riding with me, Black. You can find your own way to the museum."

I stopped dead in my tracks, mouth agape.

"How the hell am I supposed to get there?" I called out after him.

"You seem to know everything," he hollered back. "You'll figure it out."

With that, he got into his car as I ran toward him. I pulled on the passenger door handle but it was locked.

Prick.

I'd been partnered up with a genuine prick.

Graham and Fay were in his backseat. They both shrugged at me. Max strapped himself into his babyseat-looking contraption, with its multi-limbed aluminum arms and gears and pulleys that helped him drive. He threw his boat of a car into reverse and screeched off, hammering the undercarriage of his car on the parking lot ramp as he sped out.

"Okay," I yelled out to no one. "Anyone want a partner, cheap?"

I grimaced at the high pitch of my frustrated voice as it echoed back to me in the garage.

CHAPTER 11

"What's with Detective Dickhead?" Bob's voice asked from somewhere in the PPD garage. I glanced around and spotted my bodyguards emerge between two cars.

I didn't like that. That meant they saw the whole thing with Max unfold.

"You guys are being creepy," I complained. "What's up?"

"Us?" Lou asked, pressing his palms to his chest. "Whyever do you say such a thing?"

"'Whyever do'?" Bob asked, squinting at Lou. "What the hell does '*whyever do*' mean?"

"I'm asking her why she thinks we're being creepy!"

"So let me get this straight," Bob said, in that low voice he sometimes wears. The dangerous voice. It was always a sign that a fight was coming. Maybe even a violent goblin fight. "So, BB asks us why we're being creepy and your response is to answer her with crappy Shakespeare-sounding non-words? Don't you think that maybe, JUST MAYBE, that makes us creepier?"

Lou thought about this for a few seconds.

"No," Lou said, simply.

Bob smacked Lou in the head with an open hand and turned to me to continue the conversation, presumably to convince me that they were not being creepy or up to something.

Lou shoved Bob into a car.

Bob shoved Lou into another car.

They jumped on each other and started to slash away.

Goblin fights are nasty things. They're like cat fights in their viciousness, mountain goat battles in their intensity, and gorilla matches in sheer violence.

Bob and Lou had to get this crap out of their systems a few times a year.

I rolled my eyes as the sound of slashing and grunting rolled through the garage. I needed to find a ride. These two couldn't get in the way of the case.

"What the fuck is up with those two gits?" a woman's heavily-British accented voice said from somewhere behind me.

She was so short I thought she was a kid at first. Her jet black hair bobbed over her face as she glanced between me and the goblins.

"Their time of month," I replied deadpan. "You know if I can get into any of these cars? My partner drove off without me."

"Max?"

"How did you know?"

"It's what he does," she said with a shrug. "He's Max. I'm Tina."

"Bethany," I said.

"Yeah, the weretiger. Good job on the Central Park job."

"If you say so," I said. I didn't want to be impolite, but I also had to get going. "You an officer?"

"I run the garage," she said, wiping her hands on a filthy cloth.

I noticed for the first time that she was covered in oil. Even her face was smudged with black.

"Of course," I said, embarrassed that I was an officer who couldn't figure that out on my own. "So can I take any of these cars?"

She put her hands on her hips and sighed heavily as she looked around. Her pursed lips were a sure sign that I was out of luck. But then her eyes widened and she smiled a big, toothy grin.

"Got one that's a junker," she said, grinning like a champ.

"I'll take it."

"I mean a real junker. Like a Junky McJunkster's twin brother, Jasper Disaster." She chuckled. "Bad stuff, Bethany."

"Does she run?"

"If she likes you."

"I can be charming when I want to be."

She smiled at me and took a couple of steps closer, looking up at me and into my eyes a little too intensely.

"I can tell," she said with a wink. "Follow me."

We walked past the goblins who were bleeding

profusely and panting like injured animals. They didn't even know I was there anymore.

"So they *are* friends of yours, right?" Tina asked.

She threw her dirty towel over her shoulder and dug in her deep pockets.

"When they're not acting like a couple of gits." I figured I'd use some British slang to impress her.

It worked.

She laughed and tossed a set of keys over her shoulder. I snatched them from the air and spun the ring on my finger.

I spotted a rusty brown fender near the end of the lineup of cars. I hoped it wasn't the one she was taking me to, but my gut told me I was out of luck. As we approached the vehicle, it's condition got pretty damn clear.

"That runs?" I asked.

"If by runs, you mean, goes forward, yes. It doesn't do reverse." She pursed her lips. "Not without a blood sacrifice, anyway."

It was a four-door car of some kind. There was no branding. There was no paint, for that matter. Splotches of rusted metal covered the stripped exterior. The backseat passenger windows were covered in plastic sheets.

But all of that mess was nothing compared to the mess inside.

There were no backseats. The seats had been stripped out and in their place was, best I could tell, a garden. I didn't recognize the plant but its vines wrapped around the front seats like they were trying to strangle the last bit of life out of the car.

No carpet on the floor.

No upholstery on the ceiling or doors.

And the steering wheel was on the right side of the car.

I tried to hide any emotion from my face but I don't think I did a very good job. Tina smirked at me and shrugged.

"You want it?"

"How can I say no to such a fine specimen…of…car-ness."

"I like you, Bethany Black," Tina remarked with a laugh. She then popped the hood and propped it up. "First thing, if it stalls, this is your likely problem." She was pointing at a large bolt that looked ominous. "Just tighten up this bolt here and you should start back up in a jiffy. If it smokes then throw water over here and stand way the hell back." She gave me a serious look. "I mean waaaaay back, okay?"

"Okay."

"The jug of water in the backseat is for that. Hold on." She went around to the back of the car and popped the trunk, where she proceeded to pull out a small glass aquarium. A slight chattering sound came from it.

The car groaned.

There's no other way to say it. The car settled on its wheels as if it had gained a few hundred pounds in an instant. The metal even screeched and moaned.

Tina gave it a kick.

She handed me the aquarium.

It was filled with thousands of bugs. They were small,

flesh-colored things. They crawled over each other and chattered.

"What's this for?"

"The garden," she said, as if I was supposed to know what she meant. "The garden in the back of the car. When you want it to go faster or go in reverse, you'll have to feed it a bug or two. Or ten." She leaned in slightly. "One of the bugs is always a blood sacrifice, by the way, so put in at least two unless you *only* want to drive in reverse for some reason."

I checked out her face for any sign of sarcasm.

There was no sarcasm.

"Okay," I said.

She took the aquarium back and set it on the passenger seat.

I counted myself lucky to have anything, so I shoved the hundred questions about the car way down and hopped in to the driver's seat.

"You ever drive before?" Tina asked me.

"In video games," I answered.

"This should be good. It's an automatic so not much to worry about. If you need help, just ask Sue and he can give you a driving program. That should help you get to your destination. But when you get back we need to practice. I just so happen to be a driving teacher, too."

She winked at me again.

"Thanks, Tina. When those two idiots stop fighting, tell them to stay out of my way."

"You got it, Bethany Black." She said my name like it was part of a poem.

I smiled nervously at her and turned the key.

The slap on the back of my head pushed me into the steering wheel.

"What the hell?" I turned to see the vines in the backseat settle back into resting position. "What's your problem plant?"

Tina tapped on the window and pointed to the aquarium in the front seat next to me. I sighed and clenched my teeth and squinted as I snagged a couple of bugs and threw them into the backseat.

The sound of car vines eating is not something I'd expect to get used to anytime soon.

I gave Tina my best smile and pushed on the pedal that looked like the gas. I was right. Five seconds later I was driving past the battling goblins.

I glanced into the rearview mirror just in time to see them disengage, yell something, and scramble after me.

"Good luck, boys!" I yelled back as I took a left onto Delancey and enjoyed the hell out of the first minute of my driving career.

CHAPTER 12

I was damn good for a new driver. Really. No weretiger pride here.

New York is actually a great place to learn to drive. The traffic doesn't move that fast. It's mostly just a big grid until you get into the downtown area where the West Village and Wall Street areas seem to be designed to make tourists' lives miserable.

I got lucky and managed to get ten green lights on 6th Avenue. That allowed me to get to the Upper East Side in about ten minutes.

I spotted the bright lights of the Metropolitan Museum as I crossed through Central Park. Then, I turned onto 5th Avenue with a confidence that was about to go boom.

"Good job, junker," I said to the car. "You made it all the way. You mind if I call you Junker, Junker?"

For about five seconds I felt in my element. Max was testing me and my patience, but I was handling his BS just fine. I didn't expect him to be proud of me, but I was determined to smack all of his roadblocks down hard.

One second, I was racing like a pro, and the next I was doing 180s in the middle of the street.

A black car had slammed into my front left bumper. The world spun around me, turning the lights behind the street-level windows into streaks of white.

Junker crunched into something solid and came to a snapping halt. My neck jerked right and then left. My poor body was taking a beating that week. I rubbed my shoulders and tried to see who had hit me.

There were a couple of cars spitting smoke, but I knew which one to focus on instantly because three goblins threw open their doors in unison and stepped out.

They spotted me and started to run in my direction.

So, from the looks of my current predicament, I had a target on my back. And the mob was taking aim.

"I need backup!" I told Sue, the AI, through the connector.

"Max told you to stay put," Sue shot back with several hundred pounds of attitude.

I pressed down on the gas and the car jerked forward.

The jungle car was still running.

I tried to go into reverse to back away from the approaching mobsters, but the vines in the backseat unfurled and slithered around my neck and mouth. I reached for the aquarium on the passengers seat and palmed some bugs, launching them into the back. Apparently, it had already used up the original two bugs I'd fed it.

The vines unfurled and Junker rolled backwards.

At about one mile per hour.

I could have pushed it faster.

"First of all," I yelled at Sue, *"no he didn't tell me to stay put! He told me I was on my own. And two, shut your digital trap and get me backup!"*

Luckily, the bystanders kept their distance. Tried and true New Yorkers always minded their own business. One old lady shook her cane at me as I rolled by. She spit on my window.

The goblins were catching up fast. One of them stopped, planted his feet and took aim. Two of his bullets sparked off my rusty front bumper.

I unclipped my holster and slipped my 6er out.

My plan was to turn hard and fire out my window, force the mobsters to scramble, and buy some time to drive forward again.

But I yanked the steering wheel right instead of left, so I had to shoot through the passenger window instead. Hey, what can I say? I didn't get a lot of practice driving in reverse in video games.

Two of my bullets found their targets and a couple of goblins snapped back and dropped to the street. The third one turned and ran onto the sidewalk, finding cover in the shadows.

I didn't dare shoot blind. There were too many people around.

So I double-parked, told Junker to be good, and sprinted toward the museum.

I activated the connector. *"Max! Where are you?"*

"In the museum. Where are you? Lemme guess. A taxi, right?"

I spotted the goblin crossing the street to the museum. He climbed a fence and disappeared into the bushes around the side of the huge building.

"Chasing a goblin. A few of them started a gunfight with me on 88th street. I think he's headed toward you."

"I got my hands full here, Black. Call Sue for backup and take care of it."

"Thanks, partner," I hissed my reply.

"Don't mention it."

As I jumped and slid off a car trunk, I wondered how long this partnership could last.

CHAPTER 13

I dropped onto the lawn outside the museum without a sound.

We were in the restricted area surrounding the loading bay. Security cameras peered down at me from above several windows and doors. I knew the PPD was supposed to keep a low profile, but nothing could be done about it. If this goblin knew anything about the murder inside the museum, then I had to apprehend him and bring him in for questioning.

I considered doubling down on my backup request, but then I thought better of it. Why did I need help? I had one perp on the loose. I could handle a single mobgoblin.

"Sue, I've got things under control here," I said. *"Get someone to 88th Street for cleanup instead."*

"Why? What did you do now?"

"My job. Maybe you should try it some time."

"Nah, I like my life like it is. Or like it was before you showed up."

"You sending the crew or not?"

"Awright, awright, gimme a break, rookie!"

I heard a crack nearby, like glass being broken. It was somewhere ahead of me in the shadows. There were a thousand places to hide, so I did what any other PPD officer would do.

I used my abilities.

I holstered my 6er and I went full tiger.

My uniform melded with my skin as I transformed. The gun on my waist folded into my butt, just as Sir Pickle had designed. It was a weird feeling, but not as odd as the sensation of human flesh giving way to sharp tiger fur.

I scratched at my neck a couple of times and opened my senses to my surroundings. My stomach clenched as it caught a whiff of goblin meat. I'd sampled that crap on the last mission and I was in no mood to try it again.

I closed my mouth, which always opens when I'm smelling the air deeply, and ducked low. I used the brush as cover until I got to a lineup of three trash dumpsters.

There was the sound of a whimper. The goblin knew I was coming.

I let out a growl, just to solidify to him that his worse fears were coming true. Maybe I could scare him into surrendering and giving me some answers.

No such luck.

He came out of the shadows yelling…and shooting.

I leapt up onto the top of a dumpster and went as flat as I could. He had a tough time getting a bead on me from that angle. But he tried, I'll give him that.

A couple of bullets pinged off the dumpster metal.

One of them zinged right past my head. It missed me by a mere couple of inches.

If he wanted to play for keeps then I'd have to oblige him.

By my count he still had at least a few bullets left. I hoped he'd empty out his weapon, but it seemed he was too smart for that.

Too bad he wasn't so smart that he'd remember to keep his breathing under control.

He scrambled past me, sounding like he was making as much noise as humanly possible. Or was that goblinly possible?

He was making for a steep hill. Going for the high ground. I couldn't allow that.

It took a second to calculate my trajectory. Cats usually like to take our time with math. Nothing makes us happier than crunching the numbers and the angles on a perfect jump. But I only had time to do some rudimentary stuff. The rest would have to be luck.

I pushed off the dumpster with enough velocity to reach him. The question was whether I'd be able to reach him in time.

I landed with my front paws on his shoulders, shoving him down to the grass just as he reached the upward slope. From the sounds of it, his nose was the first thing to hit.

He rolled over onto his back and scrambled uphill on his butt. His nose was crunched flat from the fall and blood oozed out, shooting a stanky scent that hit my nose and eyes so hard it made me wince. I'd once read that goblin blood evolved to be as revolting to meat eaters as possible as a defense mechanism.

Well done, guys.

"Stay away!" he yelled.

He reached under his jacket and pulled out a dinky knife. It wouldn't have scared me even if I'd been a house cat.

I growled, but my job as a tiger was over.

With a thought, I changed back to human form. His eyes went wide as I popped up onto two legs, grew some shoulders, lost some fur, and pulled the 6er from the place where my butt stripes used to be.

I aimed for his bleeding nose.

He dropped the knife.

"Don't move," I warned as I opened a connection with Max.

"I have a goblin out here," I explained. *"He's alive and well, and about halfway to squealing with the right guidance."*

"That'd be great, Black, if it had dick-all to do with this mess we got on our hands in here."

"What do you mean?"

"Found a dagger. Guess what it has inscribed on it?"

I didn't have to say 'an H,' because I could hear Max say it with his smugness.

I threw handcuffs on the mobster and pulled him to his feet.

"What's your name?" I asked, as I pushed him ahead of me.

"None of yer business, bitch. OW!"

I slapped him on the back of the head. Open-handed,

which is kind of, sort of, not against the NYC PPD rules... depending on which officer you spoke to.

"Loverboy," he said.

Fresh. I slapped him again.

"It's Loverboy! That's my name!"

My brain balanced the benefits of a third slap and decided against it. He was probably full of shit, but I'd need to be cautious. I didn't feel like having too many rookie marks against me.

So I shoved him instead.

"Where we going?" he asked.

"To get some culture, punk."

CHAPTER 14

We climbed the wide steps that led up to the museum's entrance. The view of 5th Avenue would have been worth soaking in if I'd been in better company.

I laced my arm through the goblin's and did my best to avoid getting bled on. When we reached the top of the steps, I forced him into the shadows and yelled at my partner.

"Open the door, Shakespeare," I said. *"I'm outside with the goblin."*

"Are you kidding me? I'm not bringing mob to a crime scene. Just keep him there and I'll be right out."

"Why do you look like you want to kill somebody?" Loverboy asked.

My response to Max's little diatribe must have been written all over my face.

"Because I *do* want to kill somebody."

"I'll chain the goblin to the sphinx," I called back to Max. *"I can sniff out the crime scene."*

He didn't respond. I had him thinking.

"Come on, Max," I said in my calmest voice. *"Let me in."*

The rotating door unlatched and slid open.

Max stood in the lobby. He watched me push the mobster through the door and backed up, arms crossed.

"Thanks," I said, as I walked past him and immediately spotted the victim, or what was left of him.

The poor guy, a wizard from the looks of his braided mustache, was splayed out on the floor of the museum's large reception area. His chest was open and his insides ran from one end of the room to the other. One long string of red broke the tidy cleanliness of the marble floor.

Loverboy barfed.

We watched him heave up the last of his dinner until the only sound in the whole museum came from the tiny rasping lungs of a sensitive mobster.

"Sorry," Loverboy burped out. "Blood makes me…"

He heaved again.

"Yer cleaning that up," Max said to me.

"Any signs of a struggle?" I asked, ignoring him.

Max paused, glaring at me. "Yeah, he fought it out. That's what got the janitor's attention. He came running when he heard the struggle, but it was over by the time he got here."

"Is he the only normal in the place?"

"No, there are five more on the maintenance crew and six security."

"Where are they?"

"Asleep. Yer friends, the fairy and werewhatever, are guarding them."

"Why are they..."

I'd almost asked him why the humans were asleep before I remembered the answer. From the annoyed expression on Max's face, he figured out what I was going to ask. Great, another excuse for Max to call me a rookie.

"Standard protocol to send 'em to snoozieland on jobs like this, rookie. Then we call in our own normals to communicate with NYPD and City Hall."

To recover, I said, "Sorry, I just know that there are many normals who are in-the-know because of their jobs. I just assumed, this being a museum, that might be the case here."

"Nope," he replied, but the twitch of his right eye signaled that he was impressed with my comment.

"Sarge said there were two officers on the scene?"

"Biggs and Sanchez," Max answered. "They're looking around."

I nodded. "Can you watch barf boy for me?" Max's frown didn't budge, but he nodded his head slightly. "Thanks. Be right back."

I partially transformed. My nose, ears, and eyes went tiger. Not 100%, but enough for me to pick up on clues and process them with my best head on my shoulders. The only problem with pulling this stunt, is that my human brain can have a tough time sifting though all the information that my tiger senses picked up on. When it gets to be too much I have to change to tiger and just hope I retain all my best PPD officer instincts.

My boots squeaked on the shiny floor as I probed the room.

When the goblin's stomach started giving up the last

remnants of his meal, I turned and roared for him to stick a cork in it. I think the meaning was clear. Loverboy sat down and put his head between his knees.

I looked up to the top of the massive staircase that lead up to the painting gallery. The steps were 60 feet wide at their widest point and they were three stories high.

That's when I got my first hit of an out-of-place odor.

I pushed the lingering body odor of thousands of tourists aside, ignored the scent of chemicals that helped the art survive the onslaught of Manhattan's atmosphere, and did my best to filter out the stale air all around me.

One scent showed promise.

Oil.

Something mechanical was nearby. Something damaged and leaking oil. My first thought was that it was possibly Junker, but I wasn't targeting my nose in that direction.

No, it was something else. It smelled like the oil stench in the wizard's apartment.

I moved my attention to what I could hear. I listened for the sound of dripping. Maybe the oil was leaking and hitting the floor.

My instincts screamed at me that this was it. The smell meant danger. I pushed aside the urge to run. Danger was something to escape as a tiger, not attack.

I walked up the steps slowly, scanning for the slightest clue.

"You got somethin'?" Max asked.

He floated over my shoulder. I didn't hear him sneak up on me. I think the big smile on his face was proof enough that he'd wanted to do exactly that.

I nodded, glancing back down to see that he'd chained the goblin to a rail.

Then I smelled something new and my stomach clenched.

"I like you better like this," Max said. He flew ahead of me and helped me scan the area. "The whole not-speaking thing suits you fine."

I growled. The smell was getting stronger. It was all too familiar.

"And if you think about it, why do we even use words when growls will do just fine, right?"

I growled again, trying to speak the words. Trying to warn him.

He smirked at me.

But the smirk faded fast when goblins emerged from the shadows all around us.

CHAPTER 15

The museum's lobby is the size of two football fields. Its arched ceilings loom five floors high. Balconies surround the space on all sides, giving visitors a gorgeous view of the grand room below.

And giving goblin mobsters the deepest, darkest shadows to hide in.

"Good job sniffing them out, Black," Max said, sarcastically.

I didn't have a good comeback. First, because my vocal cords were half-tiger. Second, because he was right. Why hadn't I smelled a dozen goblins? My tiger nose could pinpoint a fly with bad breath in a sewer, but for some reason I hadn't picked up on the cacophony hell of goblin stench? It didn't make any sense.

But there was no time to worry about it. We had mobster asses waiting to be kicked all around us.

"Go all-in, tiger," Max shouted.

I fully transformed as I ran up the stairs. Max kept up, his little wings flapping so fast that they were a blur.

We got to the top of the staircase.

Max flew left.

I sprinted right.

I turned a corner and hugged the balcony's edge. Statues and display cases were my only cover as a few goblins took shots at me. Bullets ricocheted off the floor and knocked off a few sculptural extremities. The gunfire got so intense that I huddled behind an Egyptian sarcophagus. My ears moved around until I could hear the goblins reloading.

I took off down the long balcony hall, zig-zagging as much as I could.

The slick floor was tiled.

Not an ideal surface for tiger claws, even magical ones.

I heard gunshots from the other side of the lobby. Max had his hands full, too.

There was a lone goblin about 15 feet away. He was hiding behind a display case, mostly.

The actual goblin was out of my range for a single jump.

But the display case wasn't.

I bent my back legs and touched the floor with my chin, gripping the tile so hard with my claws that it began to crack under the stress.

Then I jumped.

It was pure luck that the mobsters' bullets missed their mark, but it was pure skill that slapped the side of the display case with my paws so hard that it fell onto the hiding goblin.

One of his hands fell onto the floor right in front of

me. I grabbed it in my teeth and yanked him hard, pulling him into the shadows.

He flailed around, trying to grab something, anything.

He screamed.

I let him.

It was a blood-curdling scream. The kind that should send a chill down the spines of his comrades.

I'd been lectured by Sarge about taking mobsters alive. He wanted me to be more merciful. I didn't see much of a reason to go light on a group of jerks who were trying to kill everyone I knew and loved, but, hey, he was the boss. The lessons he forced me to take on goblin biology were stomach-turning, but they revealed a few weak spots that would take them out without any permanent damage.

I pinned the screaming mobster to the floor with my paws on his shoulders and growled in his face. His scream went silent, but his mouth stayed open and his eyes wide. I got a glimpse of my mean face in his wide purple pupils and shivered. Not bad. I was even freaking myself out. I did what the PPD trainer taught me and shoved my wet nose into the punk's neck. The pressure interrupted the flow of slimy goblin blood to his tiny goblin brain and knocked his oily ass out.

"Bitch got Sammy," I heard a goblin say.

"Shut up and move in," came the reply.

Their footsteps grew closer and closer.

Again, I crouched and tensed every muscle in my body. If they entered my field of vision they were dead meat.

"How's it going here?" Max's voice said from behind me.

I was still coiled up like a spring, so it wasn't my fault that I swatted him across the lobby with a single slap. The goblins took shots at him as he arced through the air.

I could only hope they hadn't hit him.

"Max!" I called out through the connector.

No answer.

Shit.

"Bethany Black!" a voice yelled from the darkness.

I wasn't in any condition to answer in tiger form.

"Bethany Black!" he repeated.

Was it a trick? Did they want me to turn back to my human form for some reason? I looked around for signs of someone with a bead on me. I was slower in human form so maybe they wanted a slower target for their sniper.

"Sue, you have vitals on Max?" I asked the AI.

"Hold on," Sue said. *"Yeah, he's steady. Why?"*

"I just slapped him across the Met."

"You sure do know how to make friends, rookie."

"I didn't mean to!"

"We're not here for you!" the goblin shouted.

The voice came from a different direction. He was moving around. Probably trying to get a visual on me. I backed into the shadows.

I transformed and immediately pulled my 6er from the holster and aimed it at my best estimation of where the yelling goblin crouched.

"Okay, why are you here?" I yelled.

"We want the wizard!"

The wizard? Why did they want a dead wizard? The

mob didn't strike me as a sentimental bunch, so I doubted it was to give him a proper burial.

"This is a crime scene," I yelled. "Official PPD business. You need to throw down all your weapons and come out with your hands up."

The goblins' cackles echoed throughout the lobby. It was like a swarm of insects. From the sounds of it, they were slowly surrounding me, which meant they knew where I was.

I holstered the pistol. It wouldn't do me any good.

"That's not gonna happen, Black," the goblin said. "We've got the numbers here. Maybe it'd be smarter for *you* to throw down *your* weapon."

"She *is* a weapon, boss," said another goblin.

There was a pause. "Will you shut the hell up? I'm working here!"

"Sorry, boss."

I prepped my body to transform again, knowing that I'd have a better chance of making it out alive that way.

My tail emerged and wrapped around my side. My ears and whiskers pulled back. I was one aerodynamic supernatural, and I was ready to poke some holes in some goblins.

The next round of gunfire came from below us.

From the first floor lobby.

Someone new had joined the party.

CHAPTER 16

The mobgoblins scattered.

But it wasn't a chaotic scatter. It was like a creepy-ass dance. A well-choreographed, creepy-ass dance.

It didn't take me long to see that three of them were across the balcony from me, laying down cover fire, while another three climbed down a tapestry quickly. They hopped off and scampered through the shadows toward the corpse.

They really wanted that bloody thing.

I spotted Graham and Fay below me. They used an Information Booth as cover. The "How Can We Help You?" sign hanging from the desk was filled with bullet holes.

"You're helping just fine, guys," I said over the Connector.

"Bethany? That you?"

"Yeah, Fay, keep an eye on the wizard corpse. Goblins headed for it. Need some cover-fire in 3."

"You got it," Graham said.

"2... 1..."

I got the mobgoblin's attention by giving them a roar they couldn't ignore. Chips of marble and sparking stone flew all around me, but I kept low and moved fast. I turned the corner and came face-to-face with one of the thugs.

He smirked and took aim.

I feigned right and lunged left. His shot missed my ass by a tiger's hair.

That pissed me off.

I opened my mouth wide and showed him every one of my fangs. His little beady eyes became huge beady eyes.

He raised his gun to fire. I landed on his chest and slammed him to the hard floor. I must have knocked the air out of him because he gasped, his mouth opening and closing, as his body tried to snag whatever air it could find.

I heard a gun get thrown onto the floor. I thought that meant someone was surrendering.

But the falling statue corrected me.

A huge likeness of Medusa leaned toward me. The other mobgoblins were tipping it over.

I had to make a split-second decision. My back claws were dug into the floor's veneer. I didn't have leverage to go left or right. I had to go forward or nowhere.

So I did the only thing I could do.

I jumped toward Medusa. I grabbed onto her marble shoulder and pushed off with all the strength I had.

The statue slammed down with a sound from the apocalypse. The waves of chaos rolled through the huge lobby.

No tiger pancake for you, I thought, just before I noticed that I'd leapt off the balcony.

The lobby floor came up to meet me with no mercy. Cats always fall on their feet, but it still hurts like hell.

I bent my legs as my paws touched down. My chest hit the hard floor and I lost every bit of air I had in me.

I struggled to stay conscious. I told myself to be calm. The air would come. I just had to wait.

But I didn't have time. I heard the goblins gathering at the top of the balcony. They'd picked up their guns again.

Fay and Graham were probably reloading.

I was out of luck.

A flurry of shots erupted from the entrance and the mobgoblins on the balcony scrambled and disappeared as fast as they'd shown up.

The mobgoblins were gone.

The body was gone.

I saw Bob and Lou running toward me, guns trained on the balcony above us.

But I knew we'd failed. The goblins had outwitted us.

As the air flowed back into my system, I fought off an intense nausea. I changed back to human form.

"Hey, come on Bethany," Lou said, reaching for my arm. "You need to take it easy, kid."

I stopped and put a finger in my bodyguard's face. "I am not a kid."

I checked to be sure our Loverboy was still cuffed. But he was gone. The cuffs had been cut, probably by one of his fellow soldiers. Max would not be happy.

Shit. Max.

"Max!" I yelled.

No answer.

I opened a connection. *"Max, are you okay?"*

"Yeah, no thanks to you."

My adrenaline screeched to a halt. In case you've never had the feeling, it's kind of like being punch drunk. As if I needed that sensation on top of the missing oxygen.

"Where are you?" No answer. *"Max, where are you?"*

"Look up."

I glanced up at the ceiling but didn't see anything. I made my eyes go tiger and squinted.

A small figure wiggled in an air vent three stories up.

Max's wings were stuck in the grate. He dangled over the museum lobby, wearing the sourest face I'd ever seen on him.

Yeah, that says a lot.

CHAPTER 17

Our official backup arrived just in time.

Just in time to help me get Max unstuck.

Bob and Lou were scoping out the lobby and checking the broom closets. Sarge had mentioned that there had been reports around the city museums about small break-ins. My bodyguards weren't official PPD, but I wanted them to be useful so I asked them to check things out while I helped Max. Besides, the two goblin bodyguards had zero interest in freeing the pixie. They hated his guts and the feeling was mutual.

"Where the hell were you guys?" Max asked the backup officers.

There were four of them. I didn't know a single one, though I may have recognized a couple. I could tell they were rookies. We have a certain something about us. A certain shit-I-don't-know-what-I'm-doing-and-I-don't-know-how-to-hide-that-yet vibe.

"Sorry, Officer Shakespeare," one officer said. Her voice trembled. "We got here as fast as we could."

"Yeah? I think my grandma could have been here faster than you, and she's dead."

"I'm sorry to hear that," another officer said, as he tugged on the edge of Max's wing.

My partner hissed in pain.

"Not looking fer yer sympathy, kid. And watch the wing." He glanced at me. "What did you find, Black?"

"It looks like they used the second floor emergency exits to get in. The doors lead to an outside balcony. The blood on the floor leads to a hatch. It wouldn't budge when I tried to see where it leads."

"So, what now?" he asked.

Another test.

I could always tell when he was testing me.

"Now we find out if one of the security cameras caught anything."

Max nodded.

"WHERE?" a loud voice screamed from below us. We all jumped. I knew whose voice it was without looking.

"WHERE?" Dick, the giant EMT, repeated.

"Shhh," Max whispered at us. "Don't say a word or yer on locker room cleanup for a year."

But Dick looked up and smiled.

"THERE!"

His partner, Pat, strolled into the lobby with a gurney. The duo appeared to have a routine because it was the same one I saw at the wizard's apartment.

"Settle down, Dick." She looked up at us. We must have been quite a sight. Four rookies holding a ladder for two rookies who were trying to tug a senior officer from an air vent. "You people look busy."

"He's stuck in the air vent," I called down.

"Yeah? Huh. You think maybe we should leave him there?"

"Keep talkin', Patricia!" Max hollered.

"He's giving out locker room duty, so we're being good," I said.

"Try that shit with me, Shakespeare, and I'll leave you here with all the other relics. Dick! Get your hands out of your pants!"

"I'M MAKING MY PENIS BIG!"

Pat put her face in her hands and talked into her palms. "Private time, dude. Remember what we talked about?"

"OH, YEAH!" he said, removing his hands from his pants.

"It's getting to the point where I can't bring you anywhere. Go get the mean man down."

"He's not touching me with those hands!" Max shouted.

But Dick was already halfway up the stairs by the time Max finished his sentence. Dick strode up to the ladder, stood on the first rung, and stuck his fingers into the wall to the left and right of the vent. He yanked the whole thing out, spreading stucco everywhere.

Dick turned Max around in his huge hands and stuck out his tongue, deep in what could only be called thought. Though that word may be a slight exaggeration. It seemed to me that Dick had an innate ability to get people to safety, one way or another. An idiot savant, maybe? I couldn't really tell what his story was, or even what race he was. I'd seen him twice in two days and he'd definitely piqued my interest. As I watched Dick work, I decided I needed to know more about our resident EMT giant.

Dick held the vent up in the air and let Max dangle there for a second. Then, with massive fingers that moved slowly and gently, he flicked the edges of Max's wings until my partner dropped free.

Max settled down on the floor and brushed off. He slapped his hat on his thigh and put it back on. All in all, it was a great recovery from a humiliating situation.

"What are all of you lookin' at?" he yelled, looking up at us. "Back to HQ. Now. We have to figure out what the fuck just happened here."

CHAPTER 18

We hobbled into the briefing room with everything we had.

It took a lot of effort and a lot of caffeine to get us ready to face Sarge. His method of asking questions could be called peppering, I guess. As long as it's Cayenne pepper because that crap hurts like hell.

"He's late?" I asked whoever would listen.

"Sarge is never late," Fay said. "Something must be wrong."

"Yeah, he probably overdid the chili and espresso again," Max noted from his usual perch in the back of the room. "He's releasing a chemical attack on stall three." Fay and I shot him a look. "That's his favorite throne for some reason."

I glanced at Graham, who sat a couple of rows in front of all of us. He seemed distant again. He'd disengage from us sometimes and stare at walls, deep in whatever thoughts he carried around. Graham was still a mystery to me. I considered him a friend, but I didn't know much about him. The fact that he was deaf might have been part of our distance. I still hadn't learned to navigate regular conversation, even though he read lips so well it frequently made my jaw drop.

I poked him on the shoulder. He turned toward me and blinked and smiled, quizzically.

"You seen Sarge?" I asked.

"Nah," Graham answered. He turned in his chair to face us and leaned on the back of his seat. "He probably did his cleansing formula again and he's taking it out on stall three. He likes stall three for some reason."

"So we heard," I said.

Same Max joke, different Max.

It was just more evidence that Graham was trying to maneuver himself into a mentorship with my cranky partner. I had no problem with that. We could all learn a thing or two from Max Shakespeare, senior officer with the mysterious past.

Max looked very pleased with himself.

I realized I could probably adopt some of his mannerisms too, and he'd warm up to me fast.

Screw that.

I was going to be myself no matter what. If that meant a new partner, then so be it.

Sarge strolled in, securing his belt. Max winked at me as if to say "I told you so."

Bob and Lou followed right behind him. Had they been discussing something with Sarge? Max must have had the same thought, if the frown on his face was any sign.

"Announcement," Sarge said with zero tone in his voice. "These two are deputies now."

"What the fuck is a deputy? Like a sheriff thing?"

"Yeah, that's right, a sheriff thing, Shakespeare," Sarge said, pointing his stubby finger.

"We're not sheriffs, Sarge," Max pointed out.

His wings fluttered faster as his face got redder.

"We're whatever the higher-ups say we are. They say I'm a sheriff, then I'm a damn sheriff. And I want to be a sheriff, so I'm a sheriff. And I got two deputies now, and these are them, and that's that."

Bob and Lou stood in front of us with big grins on their faces. Each of them gave me about ten knowing winks. But I wasn't clear on what, exactly, I was supposed to know.

"Whatta we got?" Sarge asked in that booming voice of his.

"Another dead wizard," Max muttered.

"No, I asked whatta we got! And we don't have said dead wizard, am I right?"

"The mobgoblins got him," Max growled.

I could see the two of them wanted to tear into each other. Fay shot me a look, as if to say, "I'm staying out of this."

"Who was it?" Sarge asked.

Graham flipped open his notepad. "Howie Sunderland. New Jersey wizard. Owns a bar. A dive in Trenton."

"Might've been how he got swept up in mob crap," Sarge muttered.

"He's been on parole for half his life. One step away

from being sent back to the Nether. But he's been clean for five years. Parole officer loves the guy."

"Loved," Max corrected. "Any connection to the Blood Claw ritual we broke up in Central Park?"

"Nope," Graham said confidently. "He wasn't there. No relationships or known connections with the four wizards in custody."

"We got a pic of the stiff?" Max asked. Graham pulled a photo out of his notebook and handed it back. "I'll have a little talk with the Blood Claw wizards. See if I can knock some memories back in their heads."

"So why would the mob want the guy's corpse?" Sarge asked.

"Who the hell knows? Maybe he had the claw on him. Maybe his dick is made of 24-karat gold. It'd be a guess at this point."

"The mob has the Blood Claw," I said. "So killing the wizards before they use it to build their army of tiger-lites doesn't make sense."

"Unless they already made the army," Graham said.

"I'd've heard somethin' about that," Max argued.

"Or they have new wizards," I added.

Max and Sarge glared between Graham and me, like we'd pulled our pants down and crapped on their lunch.

So much for staying out of the alpha male fight.

"Why would they have new wizards?" Sarge asked.

I shrugged. "Because we have their old ones. Then again, they have this Hunter guy running around and killing them. So maybe they have some unfinished business with them."

"How do we know the museum job was The Hunter?" Max asked me.

"Because I smelled oil," I said. "I smelled the same oil on him at the wizard's apartment."

Max's face went 100%, unfiltered pissed-off. I didn't know why, but I sure did look forward to finding out.

"Why does The Hunter smell like oil?" Sarge asked.

"I don't know," I answered, "but the Sunderland wizard was definitely killed with a sharp object. Probably a knife. His guts ran thirty yards across the floor."

The silence meant they were pondering it. I joined in, wondering if I'd just said something stupid. If I did, I'd hear about it in a few seconds.

"Maybe these wizards know too much," Max mumbled.

"Yeah, the mob could be covering their tracks," Sarge said.

"We can sit here and guess all night long," Max said. "If The Hunter is taking out wizards, then we need to find out who his next target is. Graham, check on the status of the museum tapes. I want to see everything."

"Got it."

"Fay, look for a connection between our dead wizards with some fresh eyes."

"Sure thing."

"Bethany," he said, turning his frown into a weapon, "meet me in my office."

CHAPTER 19

"I didn't know you had an office," I said, trying to keep up with my partner as he zipped through the busy Main Room of NYC PPD.

He wove around the officers and the perps and the witnesses, never quite hitting them, but he got damn close. He slipped through a heavy steel door that I'd never noticed before. It led to a dark stairwell, lit just barely by flickering fluorescents overhead.

I got a glimpse of him turning the corner to another stairwell above.

After a sigh, I followed.

There was the sound of a door opening on one of the floors above me. I got to it just in time to see it click shut.

I was starting to get creeped out.

The third floor was darker than the stairwell. It was a large, empty room. It could have been a basketball court with its wood floor and high ceilings. But there were no bleachers, and the only light came from an open door on the other side of the space.

I had to step down five stairs to enter my partner's 'office.'

It was more like a pixie man-cave.

Bookshelves lined one wall. Leather-bound tomes lined up in row after row. It was the kind of collection that you'd find in a rich person's fourth home. Except in this case, I noticed how worn and read these volumes were. My partner was a reader. Interesting.

Another wall was covered in framed photographs. One of them showed Max floating just above Sarge's shoulder. Both of them clenched cigars between their teeth to form what was the closest thing to a real smile I'd ever seen on either face. Another pic's faded color dated it as really damn old. It showed a row of PPD officers, all smiling with their chests puffed out. There was a small, floating splotch on the end of the third row. I assumed it was Max. The only pixie on the force, from the looks of it. Another interesting piece of info.

I didn't get a chance to get a good look at the wall furthest away from me, though. Its tall windows were flooded with a light so bright that I had to squint.

Not that it mattered. Max was in no mood to dilly-dally.

"Don't ever do that again," he said in a terse tone of voice.

"You mean follow a strange man into a creepy room without having my gun aimed at the back of his head?"

My eyesight recovered from the bright sunlight in my face. Max was sitting at a pixie-sized desk in a small chair. It was the first time I'd seen him surround himself with things that were his size. He'd always seemed so comfortable in a world of large beings. Even his car was normal-sized. But, at that moment, he was in his element.

"Don't go into a briefing without telling me everything you know," he said.

I could tell he was pissed just by looking at his sour face. But it was a different kind of pissed in some way.

"What are you talking about?"

"You know what I'm talking about, Black."

I remembered the look he'd given me in the briefing. "What? The oil smell?"

"You didn't tell me about the oil."

"Ah," I said and then shook my head at him. "In case you hadn't noticed, we didn't have a lot of time between almost getting killed and getting to HQ for a Sarge drilling."

"*That's* your excuse?"

I marched up to him, bent down and tapped my finger on his desk as I said, "I'm not looking for an excuse! I'm looking for a break!"

"Pshhh. You came to the wrong place then."

I stared at him for a few seconds before slowly lowering myself into the cushy chair across from him.

"Like it or not, Black," Max grumbled, "we're partners. You tell me everything. If you think of something we didn't discuss then you keep your mouth shut."

"No."

He jolted. "What did you say?"

"You heard me. No."

Max stood up and slammed his fists on his desk. He clearly wanted to say something, but he held back. I waited. I was done with his shit. It was time to let it all hang out. No more dancing around the damn tension.

"You see that picture up there?" He pointed to a photo on the wall. "That's me and my last partner." A much younger Max and a handsome man were smiling at the camera. They held a medal between them. Max's partner held one side of the orange ribbon, while Max heaved up the other side. A gold medallion, as big as Max, hung between them. "That's The Valor."

The Valor medal was the highest honor a PPD Officer could receive. It was mostly given to the family of a dead officer. Living officers had to save the whole damn world to get it. I had to work hard to hide the intense curiosity.

"When we were told that one of us was going to be awarded the medal," he continued, sounding somber, "we decided that if both of us didn't get it, then neither of us wanted it. You know why?"

"Because you wanted to mess with the higher-ups as much as possible?"

"Good guess," he replied with an impressed nod, "but no. It's because we were *partners*." He paused to let that sink in. "Partners don't let *anything* get in the way. Not a woman, not a promotion, not a medal…nothing. N.U.T.H.I.N.G."

"Uh…I think you mean N.O.T—"

"*NOTHING!*" His eyes were so red that they were nearly glowing. "Partners either share or they get the fuck out."

I knew what he was saying. Hell, I *agreed* with what he was saying. But I wasn't going to be muted. Not by him, or anyone.

"I'm still not going to hold back my thoughts, Max," I stated, trying my best to keep inflection from my voice. "Ever. I'm not going to edit myself. I'm not going to change my story. I'm not going to let anything get in the way of following my best judgment in the moment. I'm your partner, yes, but I'm also a PPD officer. If I have info to share, then they need to know. Our partnership can handle a few surprises." I blinked and looked away for a moment before turning back to face him. "If it can't, then maybe we should tell Sarge to work something else out."

I couldn't tell what he was thinking. At all. His face suddenly got as blank as a lifetime poker pro.

He leaned back in his chair.

I got ready for the end of our relationship. I was ready, hoping that I wasn't going to be fired.

Then he smiled.

"Welcome to the PPD, kid."

CHAPTER 20

I didn't know what to make of the whole conversation with Max.

I wandered back to my room, sat on the bed, stood right back up, and padded out into the Main Room. I was restless, hoping to find a friendly face, but my fellow officers were too busy doing their jobs. I wanted to do mine, too, but we were in a holding pattern as we waited for test results from the crime scenes.

Bob and Lou were watching me from the balcony. They pretended to be minding their own business. I didn't feel like talking to them.

Mike.

I needed to talk to Mike.

I'd been too busy to check in with him. He was in The Zoo under heavy watch. Last I'd heard, the Director vetoed any new jobs.

Mike was to stay put until she told him he could go. He must have been going crazy being cooped up. The Zoo wasn't bad. It had all the amenities. In the final analysis, though, it was a prison. A prison for endangered races like ours. I'd been allowed to take the PPD job for reasons still unknown. The department was in dire need of recruits ever since a mage battle took out 41 officers. Still, someone had ordered The Director to let me join up. Someone with a lot of power.

Problem was, I still didn't know who that someone was.

I paced the aisles of the Big Room and dialed Mike via the connector. It wouldn't attach to Mike's connector, since he didn't have one, but it'd ring through to his cell.

"What do you want, Black?" a woman's voice said on the other line.

It was The Director.

"You took his phone?" I asked her. "Really?"

I felt my temper flaring up, but I had to be careful. I didn't want to make Mike's life any more difficult than it probably already was. Hell, I didn't want to make my life any tougher either. The Director had a million ways she could make me miserable. She could do anything she wanted in the name of protecting me, including locking me up in the Netherworld again.

"He doesn't want to talk to you," she said.

"Bullshit."

"Language, Bethany," she warned. Bitch. She let out a long sigh. "Are the boys with you?"

"Yeah, Bob and Lou are doing their job," I replied, looking up at them. "You've managed to make them miserable and creepy."

They waved at me, smiling awkwardly. I waved back but I didn't smile.

"It's for your own good, Bethany."

"So I hear. How is Mike?"

I couldn't trust her to tell me the truth, but I'd known her long enough to gauge what was real and what to ignore.

"He's not well," she sighed. My stomach dropped. "Still recovering from the… incident." Mike had been on a modeling job in New York City when he was kidnapped by the mob. Knowing The Director, she wasn't going to make the same mistake again. "His weight is back up. The area around his claw has healed, though the actual claw is obviously gone. Even with that, though, there are invisible wounds that must be treated in cases like this."

"This isn't just a case," I hissed. "This is Mike."

"Fair enough."

"I want to talk to my friend."

The pause made me think we'd lost our connection.

"Two minutes," she said. "If he gets upset it could impact his recovery."

"Fine."

There was a shuffling sound, followed by a slight cough.

"Hey BB," Mike said, his voice barely recognizable.

"Sorry I didn't call," I said.

"It's okay."

He sounded meek. He sounded scared. He sounded like someone I didn't know.

"Are they treating you okay there?" I asked, knowing that they were watching him like a hawk.

"Yeah, I guess. Just watching a lot of TV. Bored."

I'd known him most of my life. He was the only other

weretiger on the planet. We shared a bond that made it impossible to hide things from each other for long.

"Mike, what's wrong?"

"I'm…" He stopped himself.

"Is The Director there? Tell her to back off."

"No!" he yelled. "Sorry. No. She's just…she's out in the hall, okay?"

"Okay." I had to be gentle.

I wasn't going to push him on this. If he wanted to talk, then he'd talk. I could feel him struggling, trying to think of what to tell me. I wanted the truth. I couldn't help him if he didn't tell me the truth.

I'm not sure how long we sat in silence. It was long enough that I was surprised to hear him break the silence.

"I'm scared, BB, that's all."

"It's over, Mike. You're safe."

He laughed. It wasn't just a chuckle either. I waited for him to stop.

It was during that wait that I understood the size of the problem.

Mike was fragile.

My stomach clenched.

I sensed danger for him. My instinct was to wrap my arms around him until he felt better. I dreaded what he would say next. Whatever it was, it was going to be a lot to digest. The laughter finally died down to nothing. But Mike was silent.

I reached my room and slipped in, closed the door gently and sat on my bed.

Then, I whispered, "Mike?"

"I'll never be safe," he said. "You either. We're targets now, Bethany. You can see that, right?"

It would have been easy to say something like, 'The Zoo is the safest place in the Nether,' or 'The kidnapping was a one-time thing,' but he'd know I was stretching it. The fact was, I hadn't thought of it that way. We'd saved Mike from being pulled to pieces by the mob and its wizards, and my brain stopped there. I hadn't considered the bigger picture. Sure, the one claw we were trying to chase down could be recovered, yeah. But, so what? Then they'd just come for Mike again. And again.

Or they'd come for me.

What the hell was I doing in my room, whispering through my connector?

Why wasn't I out on the streets, hitting every mobgoblin hangout until our next step made itself clear? Why were we waiting on lab tests? Why were we being so cautious?

"You there, BB?" Mike's voice broke me out of my growing rage.

"I'm here, Mike. You just take care of yourself."

"But you need to get back here. You're in danger."

I paused as my jaw tightened. "I signed up for this. You know that."

"I want you here."

"And I want to be there, too," I replied, which kind of freaked me out since it was the truth, "but you're right, Mike. There's only one way we can ever be safe again."

"Bethany, you're freaking me out. Promise me you won't do something stupid."

"Who do you think you're talking to?" I asked. "Stupid is my middle name."

He chuckled, but it was forced. He was worried. I was worried. But I could do something about it.

A few seconds ago, I'd been worried about what Mike was going to say. I knew it would change my world. And it had. My world was now more terrifying. But my goal was clear.

It was either me and Mike, or the mobgoblins.

Only one of us could survive.

I wasn't going to stop the next Blood Claw ritual. I wasn't going to fight whatever armies they could concoct.

I was going to destroy them before they destroyed me and mine.

My purpose was clear.

The mob had to be destroyed.

CHAPTER 21

I suited up and stormed out of my room with enough energy to power Sir Pickle's lab for a year.

And I ran into Bob and Lou.

My bodyguards were as surprised as I was as they slid across the floor and came to a stop at Graham's feet.

"What the hell are you doing outside my door?" I yelled. "Were you listening to my conversation?"

"No!" Bob yelled, getting up and wiping himself off. "Fuckin' A, BB, we were just about to knock on your door."

Graham stepped over Lou and handed me a yellow slip. "Some results came back from toxicology."

I collected myself and tried to make sense of the words on the paper.

Tx: .007 yeast filler

Tx (secondary): Inconclusive. Trace (.0001) Toxicodendron radicans

Origins: American beer (all), wheat products such as bread, goblin beer (secondary), poison ivy

Outliers: Poison ivy

"Poison ivy?" I asked. "The wizard had a rash?"

"In his guts, I guess," Graham said.

"What do you mean?" I was trying not to be an asshole, but Graham's frown showed me I was not succeeding.

"I mean that the poison ivy was inside him."

"He was eating poison ivy?"

"If he drank goblin beer, yeah," Lou said as he stood on his tip-toes and peeked at the slip of paper in my hand. "Goblin beer has poison ivy."

"Jesus, why?" I asked.

"Gives it that little kick," Lou said with a grin. A grin that disappeared when he realized I didn't have time for joking around. He cleared his throat and looked at the floor.

"Seriously?"

All three of them nodded.

"So where do they serve goblin beer?" I asked, but I knew the answer before Lou offered it up.

"Jonny," we said together.

Max and I had shaken down their bouncer on the Blood Claws case.

"Does Max know?" I asked.

"He's the first to know," Graham said. "Every time."

I suspected that Graham had been sure to show Max the report before anyone else. Getting on Max's shit list wasn't fun, and the fastest way there was to keep him out of the loop on something.

I opened a connection with my partner. *"Where are you?"*

"None of yer goddamn business."

"We need to get to Jonny. Lab reports came back and..."

"I know all of this, Black."

"Then why aren't we on our way now?"

"What the hell crawled into your milk bowl?"

I clenched my teeth and stopped myself from saying all the things I wanted to say, all of them bloody and violent. Getting on Max's shit list may have been bad, but getting on mine wasn't exactly a party either. Max was already taking up slots one through four.

"Where are you goin?" Bob called after me.

"To Jonny's bar."

"I don't think that's a good idea," Lou piped in.

"I don't think I asked you if it was a good idea." Those two were positions five and six. "You coming, or not?"

I turned to face the boys and Graham. They looked at me and then at each other.

"Fine. Later."

I ran down the steps to the underground garage. Tina smiled and waved as I passed by, and she didn't ask any stupid questions. I liked her.

"Hey, Junker," I said as I plopped in the car.

The vines slithered around the backseat. I snagged a few bugs from my supply in the glove box and tossed them back to fire the ugly thing up.

I was pulling out of my spot when Bob and Lou fell through the door and ran at me.

My first thought was to just drive out of there, leaving them behind, but I could use their help. I was headed into mobgoblin territory. Maybe they could help me extract some info from Jonny, the goblin bouncer, who was known for being an idiot. The kind of guy who knew a little bit about everything and a lot about nothing. He was a handful. He'd put a gun to Max's head the last time we met.

If he tried that on me, I'd have to use a lot of energy to stop myself from opening his arteries and enjoying the show.

Yeah, I was feeling hot under the collar. I was determined. I knew that I was being reckless. I knew that leaving Max behind would end up getting me in trouble. And I knew that I didn't really give a shit at the moment.

But Mike's voice echoed through my head like a thought and a memory, and a concern and a premonition all at the same time.

I'll never be safe.

I wanted to prove him wrong, but that meant seeing the big picture. We couldn't just find the claw and put some mobsters in jail. We had to bring the whole operation down.

I was in a hurry to move.

A surge of energy flowed through every muscle. It was like I could feel my claws digging into my enemy. I looked down at my hands and they were paws, magical claws out.

Whatever Max was up to, it wasn't as important as getting this party started.

"Jeez, BB," Lou said as he hopped into the front seat. "What the hell is wrong with you? Slow down!"

Bob made for the backseat, spotted the writhing vines through the backseat's window, and turned right back around to get in the front with his cousin. The two goblins scrunched together and managed to get the door shut. Mostly.

"Nothing is wrong with me," I said without inflection. "We have a clue. I'm following it."

Then, to prove that something was definitely wrong with me, I slammed the gas and peeled out.

Junker backfired a couple of times.

We hit the avenue at a cool one mile per hour.

Bikes were passing us on the left and right. An old lady passed us while speed-walking her chihuahua down the sidewalk.

"Um, maybe we should take the subway?" Lou said and asked at the same time.

"Just pull out some bugs," I said with a slight growl on the end.

"Bugs?"

"There. In the glass case."

"I'm not touching bugs," Lou said, glancing at Bob.

"Don't look at me, numb nuts."

"Oh, for fuck's sake." I grabbed a handful of Junker snacks and launched them into the backseat.

Bob and Lou went wide-eyed as they turned back and watched the plant crunch away.

We bucked a couple of times, sending us forward and back, and then we shot off like a bullet. A 25 mile per hour bullet, sure, but it was bullet speed for Junker.

"Dammit, rookie, where the hell did you go?" Max yelled over our connection.

"We're on our way to Jonny, like I said. You joining us or do you still have better things to do?"

"Better things to... why you... kitty-litter-eating, hairy-faced, mental MIDGET!"

"You talking to Max?" Bob asked me. I guess my finger-whitening stranglehold on the steering wheel gave it away. I nodded. "He pissed?"

"That's one word for it," I said.

"If you bothered to give me three minutes, we could have done this right!"

"We don't have three minutes, partner," I argued. *"We need to get going. We don't have time to wait for you to do whatever you were doing. Which, by the way, I wasn't given any information on. You bitch and moan at me constantly about telling you every detail of what I'm doing, but do you give me that same courtesy? No, you don't. Partner."*

"Okay, fine," he growled. *"You want to know what I was doing, Black?"*

"Of course I want to know, Max," I shot back. *"You're the one constantly saying that we tell each other everything. According to you,* not *telling each other everything kills our chances of success. So, of course I want to fucking know what the hell you were doing!"*

"I was taking a crap, you moron!"

Damn.

My grip loosened on the steering wheel and my shoulders slumped so fast that the seat squeaked.

"Oh," I said, after a few moments. *"Sorry. Meet you there?"*

He'd broken off the connection.

Maybe he had been taking a crap. Maybe not. But one thing I knew for sure was that I was in deep shit.

The tiger pride had bared its fangs again.

CHAPTER 22

"That car needs someone to put it out of its misery," Bob muttered after he made sure he was a safe distance away from Junker.

"I like it," I said.

"We all like our first cars," Lou said with a beaming smile. "Mine was a Datsun."

"You hated that thing!" Bob yelled.

"I didn't hate it." Lou was frowning. "I mean, sure, we had a complicated relationship. The courting didn't go well, but we figured it out."

Bob and I stared at Lou, expecting him to clarify what the hell he was talking about.

"What?" Lou asked, shrugging his shoulders.

"Where the hell is he?" I asked, scanning the area for Max.

"Ask him."

"He's not answering. Big baby."

"You *did* leave him with his dick hanging out," Lou said. "Literally."

"Spare me that picture in my head, please," I grimaced. "He's got one minute and then I'm heading in."

"See, that's the kind of decision you should think twice about," Max's voice said from above us.

Had he flown to the bar this time? He usually drove his tub of a car. Badly. Maybe he needed to clear his head with some fresh New York City air? A quick scan of the area showed that he'd parked down by one of the garbage bins. Fitting.

"Excuse me?" I asked, sounding bitchier than I'd intended.

"That 'he's got one minute and then I'm heading in' bullshit, rookie. Whenever you lay down ultimatum crap like that, there should be a little voice in yer head that says, 'Hey, jackass, settle down.'"

"I already have a little voice in my head telling me that," I said, crossing my arms and giving him a look that conveyed *he* was source of the little voice. "It's an incessant, nagging, tinny voice that drones on and on about my shortcomings."

"Yeah, well I have better things to do than to babysit you, so get your own damn voice." Max pointed at Bob and Lou. "You two stay outside."

"Deputies," Bob and Lou said together as they pointed their thumbs at their faces.

Max sighed and flew past me toward the bar's graffiti-covered door in the alley behind us.

"They're your responsibility," Max said to me and then he knocked on the door.

Shave and a haircut. Again. Why the hell was everyone planting that song in my head?

"Responsi..." Bob sputtered. "We're not her responsibility! She's our responsibility!"

Max glanced over his shoulder. His eyes were at half-mast. He looked like an asshole librarian giving the sneezer in the reading room the evil eye. "Great job so far, goblin."

"Hey, she's alive, isn't she?" Lou shot back.

The door opened and Jonny peeked his long-ass nose out of the darkness. His beady eyes stopped on me and the nose attempted to retreat back into the shadows.

Too bad I'd grabbed the tip of it and yanked him out into the alley.

"HEY!" the mobgoblin yelled. "Watch the nose, cop!"

"Yeah, the chicks dig the nose," Max said with a chuckle.

"Yeah, Shakespeare, they *do*." He rubbed his schnoz. "What the fuck are you two doing here?"

"Hey!" Bob said, puffing his chest out. "Four."

"Who is this?" Jonny asked with a gulp.

His demeanor changed. He looked scared. He didn't fear a beating from his favorite cops, but he did fear the presence of a couple of goblin strangers.

"They're not mob," I said.

Max shot me a dirty look. He probably didn't want to give that info away. He liked to use info like a weapon.

"Not anymore," Lou said, glaring at Jonny.

"Maybe," Bob added.

"We need to ask you some questions," I said. "Quick, easy. We get the info, we leave. No fuss."

"You really are a rookie aren't ya?" Jonny asked. "Come on, then. Let's get this over with."

We followed him into the dark bar.

It was before hours, so the place was empty. I wondered if the bar was just a front for something more sinister in the back room. I turned my nose slightly tiger and I sniffed around while Jonny mumbled something like, "…forbid they call first… same shit… just trouble and trouble… did I turn off the stove?"

He threw open the door to the basement and gestured for us to go down the stairs. Max slapped him on the back of the head. Jonny sighed and went first.

It was the same routine we went through last time. I was surrounded by creatures of habit.

The basement had a single bulb hanging from the ceiling. The dim light gave us enough to work with.

"How can I put my neck on the line for you assholes this time?"

"Poison ivy beer," I said. Jonny gave me a look.

"Psssh, yeah? So?"

"You serve it here."

He furrowed his brow. "All goblin bars serve it."

"You're the only goblin bar within a thousand miles."

"So what?"

"It was found inside a wizard," Max said.

"Inside a…" He paused as his face went sour. "You guys getting kinky on me now? I ain't into that shit, got it?"

"A dead wizard, jackass," Max grunted.

Jonny processed this for a moment and then his eyes widened as delicious realization flowed through that tiny brain. He smiled at his own deductive reasoning before noticing all of us were staring at him.

"What?" He said, shifting uncomfortably in his seat. "I knew that."

"Why would a wizard drink that stuff?" Max asked. "Goblins and wizards don't tend to socialize over a drink."

"Used to be that way, yeah," Jonny admitted. "Now we see wizards come and go all the time. Last few months I've seen more of them than of my own damn kind, truth be told."

"What changed?" I asked.

Jonny shrugged. "Business probably."

"Business."

"Yeah. Business. Transactional developments of the progressive kind." Suddenly Jonny sounded like he had a brain. Maybe there was more to him than I thought. "I assumed that one of ours needed their kind to get some shit done, know what I'm sayin'?"

"Assume I don't," I said. I wanted to extract as much info as I could out of this guy before he pulled one of his standard getaway attempts.

"Look, lady. Sometimes we don't have the skills to get shit done that others do have. When such an occurrence occurs, well, you spend the money to get it done."

"You're saying a lot without saying anything," I pointed out.

That confused him. He started to mouth my words with his lips. I could tell he was trying really hard to figure out my point. So much for him having a brain.

"Meaning, that you haven't told us dick all about what kind of business the goblins might have needed," I explained with some heat.

"Hey, back off, cop." Jonny took a couple of steps back

and held his hands out like I was about to attack him. "Only so much I can say before I risk losing the blood in my body. Catch my drift?"

"How's yer uncle?" Bob asked out of the blue.

Jonny's eyes went even wider than before. Then he frowned at my bodyguards.

"Who you talkin' about?" he replied to Bob. "What uncle? Get the fuck outta here, you don't know my uncles."

"Uncle Guido," Lou added.

Bob smirked at Jonny's face and smiled. He looked over at Lou and gave him a quick nod. Lou nodded back.

"Whuh… But… huhhuh," Jonny managed to push through his vocal cords.

"What language is that, Lou?" Bob asked.

"Whuh but huhhuh?" Lou repeated Jonny's 'words.' He then rubbed his chin thoughtfully while looking off into the distance. Finally, he snapped his fingers and said, "Sounds like OhShitI'mScrewed-ese to me."

"Could be, could be," Bob said nodding his head. "Would be a fitting time to use it, rare as the dialect is these days."

"Yep."

"Look, guys," Jonny said as he slowly reached back and leaned down toward the boxes behind him, "I'm not sure if—"

I kicked his feet out from under him as Max tipped the boxes over to reveal a pistol.

"It's like you never learn," Max sighed. "Didn't we do this last time we were here, Officer Black?"

"It is *really* familiar," I said, "but the big difference this time is that I get to be the bad cop." I put my foot on the goblin's chest and kept him down, digging my heel into his solar plexus. "So tell us what kind of business the last wizard who walked through that door was looking for." I bent forward and met his pained eyes. "Or we call Uncle Guido."

CHAPTER 23

The four of us had never worked well together. Max hated Bob. Or Bob hated Lou. Or I hated Max. Or Max hated everyone and everything he'd ever come into contact with.

But extracting the scoop from Jonny as a team felt really good.

To us, mind you, not Jonny.

I got my first glimpse at what we could do together. Sure, scaring the crap out of a goblin was a one-person job. But we'd worked together.

Maybe we'd work well together again.

The light silence in the car only needed a small spark to ignite.

"You don't know his Uncle Guido do you?" I asked.

"Good guess, huh?" Bob said.

We laughed and the silence was gone.

Once we calmed down, we reviewed the whole interrogation all the way to our destination. The boys kept laughing and slapping their knees. Lou slapped the seat once by accident, in a fit of laughter, and the car hit him back with a vine to the back of the head.

I only managed to get a few seconds of glee before I felt the stubbornness coming back. It diluted the laughter. It made me focus on what we needed to do.

Jonny's tip had better be on the money, or I'd go back and find out how strong a goblin sternum was.

We pulled into the outdoor lot on the corner of Avenue A and 11th Street. Junker shot out a couple of backfires and made a few car alarms go off.

Max was already there.

"What the hell took you so long?" he asked, leaning against his front tire and smoking a cigar. He pushed his hat back on his head and squinted up at me.

"Look at my car, Max," I said.

He did. I couldn't be sure he actually saw the car through all of the smoke. "Yeah? Better than the car I had when I joined the force."

"What did you get?"

"Nothin'."

"Clever."

"In fact," he added, "I don't recall giving clearance for you to have yer own vehicle."

"Hey, you told me to find my own way to—"

"I know what I told you," he interrupted. "That doesn't mean you get your own car."

The car made a noise.

"Did that thing just growl at me?" Max asked, moving back.

I shrugged. "This is the place?"

"That's it," he said, keeping one eye on Junker.

We were standing at an old warehouse. Its broken-out windows were as dark as the night sky.

Jonny had claimed that one of the wizards who had been in the bar brought a friend. Another wizard who fit the description of the heavily-mustachioed museum corpse, Howie Sunderland. They drove a van with Petunia Plumbing, LLC painted on the doors. Jonny remembered the name because that was his mom's name.

The painted Petunia's Plumbing sign loomed over us.

From the looks of the warehouse, business was not good.

We followed Max through the shadows and stopped in front of a set of docking bay doors. Max put a finger up to his lips and shot up into the air. He hovered in front of some broken windows and peeked inside. He dropped back down on us fast and almost hit the ground, but he fluttered his wings at the last possible second.

My partner, the daredevil.

"It's dark as shit in there," Max noted.

"Is shit dark?" Bob asked.

"Don't fuckin start, Kitten Tail."

"Actually," Lou said, "shit can be very light before it hits water."

Bob blinked. "And you know this how?"

"Camping."

"You've never camped in your life and you know it."

"Yeah, yer right." Lou said, looking away.

"What?" Bob said. "What are you hiding from me? I know that fuckin' look, Lou."

"Nothin'! Jeez! Nothin'!"

He was lying. So…so…badly was he lying.

"You *have* been camping before," Bob said, apparently changing his mind. "You went camping with Granny G, didn't you?"

Uh-oh.

"We do not have time for this shit," Max said.

"No, camping with…" Lou opted to add a fake laugh to the end of that sentence.

Now he was convincing exactly zero of us.

Lou was a favorite of their grandma, Granny G. The G stands for Goddamn-it-get-me-out-of-here. If you met her you'd see it's the perfect name for her. Bob was more than a little jealous of his cousin's warm relationship. Well, not warm. But close to zero degrees, which is warm for Granny G.

"Where did you go camping?" pressed Bob. "The fuckin' Bronx? Granny hates nature!"

"We didn't…" stuttered Lou. "It wasn't like—"

"Where?"

Max cursed under his breath and tried to lift the cargo doors on his own. I rolled my eyes and helped him. So much for a stealth entrance. Max shot me a look as if this was all my fault. All I could do was shrug.

"Did you just say Westchester? Granny G went to Westchester? She tells everyone she's never left New York City!"

"She's lying, okay? That what you want me to say? I was like ten years old, Bob!" Lou was now facing Bob directly. "It's not like I could tell her to fuck off, right?"

"You coulda!"

The door rose a little bit.

"Guys," I whispered with a hissing tone. "Guys! Help us!"

"I wouldn't be standin' here with you right now if I did," Lou said as he and his cousin walked and whined together.

"That sounds kinda nice, actually, when you put it that way," Bob said with enough venom to kill a snake.

"You know what? If you want Granny to be nicer to you then maybe you should be nicer to..."

The doors slid up fast and made enough sound to wake the city.

A dozen mobgoblins stood on the other side of the door, barely lit by the street lamps behind us.

But all of us could see the tommy guns aimed at us.

CHAPTER 24

It was a setup.

Jonny had set us up.

That jerk's sternum was going to feel the full fury of my foot as soon as I saw him again.

Max flew straight up. I went Full Tiger and jumped right. Bob and Lou tried to jump on top of me, but missed me by about 30 feet.

Tigers are fast.

The sound of a gun going off is scary. The sound of a gun firing at you is terrifying beyond words. Your body almost expects to feel itself get torn apart.

I landed on top of a car just outside the garage door. The mobgoblins emerged from the darkness with their machine guns ready to go. They spotted me and turned in unison to fire.

I half-jumped, half-slid off the car and landed behind it. Bullets ricocheted off the pavement at my paws, sending sparks flying all around me.

I was cornered.

"She's trapped," I heard a mobgoblin whisper. "You go right, we're left. You stay."

"Max," I said through our connection. *"Now would be a good time to use the firearm on your person."*

"I was about to say the same thing," he replied. *"I'm surrounded, too."*

"Where are the boys?"

"Kitten Tails? Who the hell knows? Ran back home to Granny G?"

I didn't have time to tell him to shut it. The black shoes of the mobgoblins slid into view. The acrid stench of shoe polish flowed into my nose.

There was only one chance of getting out of there alive.

"Where did she go?" I heard a mobgoblin say as he turned the corner of the car.

Their little shoes on both sides of the car stopped short.

I'd changed back to human form at the last second so I could fit under that stupid small car. They were expecting a frontal attack from a fanged beast, but they got a stealth attack from an armed officer instead.

And it had worked.

I had my 6er ready to go, and I shot six shins before they knew what hit them.

Yay me.

I was sure Max would be so proud of me. Kidding.

"Those your gunshots?" Max asked.

"Yeah."

I heard guns fire from the other side of the warehouse.

"Those your gunshots?" I asked.

"Yup."

"You winning?"

"I'm always winning."

I snagged a few tommy guns from the pavement around me and slid them under the car with me. I reached for the last one and someone shot at my hand. Just missed. Shrapnel cut into my cheek.

"I got him," Lou said from somewhere nearby.

I heard a loud thud and a goblin fell to the pavement, out cold. I watched his tongue slowly roll out of his head as his eyes crossed and then shut.

"Thanks," I said to Bob and Lou as I crawled out from under the car.

"Yer welcome," Bob and Lou said together.

Bob held a broken beer bottle. Lou held his shoe. They glared at each other. I could tell they were about to get into it again.

"Guys, not now. You can argue about who knocked him out later. Okay? Please?"

They mumbled and grumbled. Bob threw the bottle over his shoulder as Lou skipped on one foot and tried to slip back into his shoe.

Max swooped down from the night sky and cuffed the injured goblins to each other. I handed him my cuffs to wrap up the last two.

"Stop whinin', gobbies!" Max yelled. "You jerks got off easy. Fuckin' cowards. Yer buddies who surrounded me didn't just take one in the shin, know what I'm sayin'?" He flew in front of one of them and glared. "So how did you know we were comin'?"

The mobgoblins just shot him the evil eye, lips clenched shut.

"Fine. Yer all headed back to the Nether anyways, so keep yer secrets. We'll find out sooner or later."

"I think we already know how they heard about us," I said.

Max looked at me sideways and sighed. "Yeah."

"You cops got it all wrong," one goblin said between short breaths. His squeaky voice made my ears hurt.

It was the goblin who escaped us in the museum.

"Hey, Loverboy," I said.

Max looked at me like I was nuts.

"What?" I said. "That's his name."

"We don't need to know when yer comin'," Loverboy whined. "You need to know when we're comin'."

"Is that so?" Max asked with a voice so sharp it made me flinch.

"Yeah," the goblin said. "That's so." But he didn't look as cocky as Max flew up to his face.

"If yer talking about yer little army yer buildin', I got somethin' to tell you, dipshit. We know all about it. We know who's behind it. We know how it's done. We know how to stop it." Max was lying, but it was worth it to see Loverboy's face. The goblin's eyes went wide. Max smiled at his response. "And now we know that you're senior enough to know about the plan, too. Yer comin' with us. Officer Black, will you do the honors?"

I smirked as I bent over to lift the mobgoblin to his feet. "You need to work on your poker face, dude," I said. He flinched as I stuck him in the front seat of Junker. "Don't bleed too much. It might make the car hungry."

The vines in the back seat squirmed and let out a low whistle. I didn't know what it meant, but it definitely sounded dangerous.

Loverboy looked up at me, pleadingly. I almost felt sorry for the guy. Almost.

A black van pulled up to a nearby curb, and some officers got out. A couple of them grabbed small gurneys.

"You called for medics already?" I asked Max.

"No. You didn't?"

I shook my head.

"Sue," Max called in the connector, *"how did backup get here so fast?"*

"How do you think, asshole?" Sue said.

"Sue, so help me..."

"I sent them because you two jerkoffs need medics everywhere you go. Got it?"

Max sighed and closed the connection. He flew past me and muttered, "Yer a bad influence on me, kid."

CHAPTER 25

The medic gave our mobgoblin a salve for his wound. I'd barely nicked the jerk, but you'd think I'd taken his leg off from his whining.

Driving three goblins through the streets of New York is not something I want to do ever again. The smell alone will haunt me forever. Bob and Lou did their best to keep it clean, but my nose could always pick them up.

The mobgoblin smelled like he took a bath in gray water.

It was so bad, I went to roll the window down. It was freezing outside, but I couldn't take it anymore.

The window didn't move.

I sighed, grabbed a few bugs, and threw them in the backseat.

The window opened.

I rubbed my face and tried to compose myself.

"Where you takin' me?" Loverboy asked.

"We're going to visit a friend of ours and he's going to identify you for us...after I kick his ass."

I mumbled the last part.

I guess I shouldn't have been surprised that Jonny had sold us out. He was no friend of the PPD. But he must have known we'd come back for him once we found out he'd squealed on us. It's one thing to throw us under a bus, but it was quite another to throw us in front of a dozen armed mobgoblins.

"This'll blow his cover, BB," Lou said. "Max won't be happy you outed his fence to this joker."

"No one's breaking cover today," I replied. "I'll make sure he keeps his distance. Loverboy won't see anyone."

"Why they call you Loverboy?" Bob asked. "You got a way with the ladies?"

"You could say that, yeah," the little creep muttered. A small smirk cracked his face and it made me shiver.

"Not a lot of ladies where yer headed," Bob said.

"I'll get free again. My boys always know where I am."

"Yeah, we'll be ready for them this time," I said as I turned onto Delancey.

The plan was to stop a couple of blocks away from the bar and bring Jonny close enough to see Loverboy from the shadows. He may have known the perp by name but we didn't have time to go back and forth. I needed an identity on this guy so we could interrogate him, and I needed it fast.

I backed Junker into an alley and shut off the lights.

"You guys keep an eye out. I'll be right back. You see anything weird, drive out of here."

"In this thing?" Lou asked, pointing his thumb at the plant life in the backseat.

"You can handle Junker. Just feed him if he acts up." I patted the roof a couple of times and closed the door.

The streets were crowded. It was a Friday night in the Lower East Side. Lots of bridge and tunnel kids, as they call partiers from Jersey. I fit right in with my black leather jacket, boots and jeans, recently ripped by the rough pavement of New York.

"Hey sweetheart!" a guy yelled from behind me.

My gut jumped and my fist clenched.

It was not a good time to mess with me. I walked faster.

"Hey, hey, hey," he said as he caught up to me. He was drunk. He was 18, max. And he was with his buds. Bad combo. "What's the rush? You late for your photo shoot? Cuz you are fine, sweetheart."

I stopped walking and closed my eyes.

I had to control my temper.

I had to control the urge to show this asshole what his left nut looked like. By dangling it in front of his screeching face.

That would be fun.

For me.

I took a deep breath and turned to face him.

"Sorry, not interested. Don't follow me."

He glanced over his shoulder and his boys hooted. His jerky smirk barely hid the desperation.

"Look," I whispered, "you have to save face, right? You made your move, and now you conquer or you lose cred. Right?"

His smirk faded and he put his hands in his pockets. "Well… yeah, I guess."

"I'm going to do you a favor," I said, reaching into my pocket and getting out my notepad, "but you have to do me a favor, too."

"You got it, sweetie," he said.

"First, shut the fuck up on the sweetheart, sweetie shit."

"Totally," he said as he watched me write something on the paper, curious.

"Second, don't do this to another woman. Ever. You do, and I'll find you."

I lifted my jacket and showed him the 6er. His eyes went wide.

"This is my turf," I explained slowly. "If I see you chase another woman down the street, I'll make you dickless. Got it?"

"Yes, ma'am."

I handed him the slip of paper and put my hand on his cheek. His buds hooted and hollered. As far as they were concerned, I'd just given him my number.

"And you keep an eye on them, too," I warned him, eyeing his pals. "I've never seen a single man look happy when I've removed his nuts. Do you catch what I'm saying?"

He gulped. "Yes, ma'am."

I walked away. Fast. That was wasted time.

"I think I love you," the guy yelled after me.

I closed my eyes and controlled the urge to slap him.

The screech of tires getting ahead of themselves filled the narrow streets. Two black cars turned onto Delancey.

I watched the first one pass by and yelled, "Slow down, asshole!" like a good New Yorker.

But the second car shut me up fast.

Jonny sat in the backseat between two big goblins. I recognized them as members of Frankie's crew, from back when we had our little party at The Subway, a messed-up nightclub on Wall Street.

"Max," I said after opening a connection, *"we've got a problem."*

CHAPTER 26

Junker started right up.

He didn't even need to be fed. He must have sensed the urgency and decided to throw me a bone.

We screeched out of the alley, just in time to spot the second black car turn onto 1st Avenue, heading south.

They were going for the bridge.

"I'm on 1st Avenue," Max said. *"Talk to me."*

"They're headed for the bridge. We're both behind them. Any PPD near the bridge? Maybe we can cut them off."

"Sue?" Max asked.

"How can I do your job for you now?" Sue droned.

"Anyone near the Manhattan Bridge?"

"Yeah, you two bozos."

"Anyone else, Assface?"

"Just Beat."

"Who's Beat?" I asked.

"Officer Beat. She's NYPD, but she's one of us."

"We have a mole in NYPD?"

"She's a diplomat. A gesture of good will to City Hall."

"You guys do things different in New York," I said, recalling all the news specials I'd watched on the PPD while growing up.

"You finally catching on, huh?" Max laughed. *"I'm looping her in."* A second later, he said, *"Beat, you there?"*

"Shakespeare?" said a woman's voice in response. *"What the hell do you want?"*

"You near 1st?"

"I'm on a date, but I'm over by 1st, yeah."

"We need a wind spell on two cars. Gotta stop them before they get to the bridge."

I'd never heard a sigh over the connection before. It hurt my ears.

"Fine. What am I lookin' for?"

"Two black cars, right on each other. One is—"

"I see 'em," she interrupted.

"Thanks, Beat." Max said. *"I owe you one."*

"You say that every time and I've never once gotten a 'Thank You' card."

"I'll send you a card!"

"Sure you will. Fill it with money."

I wove through lines of cars and ran a couple of red lights. I knew I'd get in trouble if I was stopped by the police, but I was willing to take the chance. There was too much at stake to let our main fence get dead.

I saw the headlights in the sky before I heard the wind.

"Is that a car up there?" Bob asked, pointing into the night sky.

A wind roared past us, making Junker shake and rattle.

"Two cars," Lou added.

The vehicles twirled in circles.

Then they flew toward us.

There wasn't time to get out of the way.

I knew I could escape. I was fast enough to be a half-block away in a second, but I couldn't leave the boys there to die.

"Get out!" I yelled, right before a car slammed down on the median next to us.

The second car crashed down onto its trunk.

Car alarms from all over the neighborhood blared in the stunned silence of 1st Avenue.

"You guys keep the normals away, okay?" I said to Bob and Lou.

They nodded their heads, unable to speak after almost being crushed by two flying cars.

I got out of Junker and ran to the black cars.

Mobgoblins stirred in their seat belts and air bags.

Jonny wasn't in the first car.

I ran to the second one and pulled the back door open.

My stomach dropped.

No Jonny.

They'd swapped him out.

I popped the trunks on both cars. Still no sign of our goblin.

Max appeared over my shoulder.

"He's gone," I said.

He scratched his head. "When would they have had time to get rid of him?"

"I don't know. It was maybe one minute, Max. It doesn't make any sense."

"Speaking of any sense," he said, "any *scents*?"

"Haha," I replied, blandly.

I partially transformed. My nose picked up Jonny's scent. It was strong.

"It's like he's here, but he's not here," I mused.

"What's that mean?"

"If I went on scent alone, I'd say he was in this car, right now."

Max looked inside again. "He's not."

"I know that. It's just weird."

My eyes told me we'd lost Max's favorite turncoat, but my nose told me to poke around some more.

One of the mobgoblins opened his eyes and moaned.

"What happened?"

"You lost your charge," I answered. "Where's Jonny?"

"Who? The snitch?" He sat up straight and grabbed his neck in pain. "He was right here."

"You'd better tell us, gobbie, or we tell him yer not cooperatin'." Max pointed to Loverboy, who sat in Junker, his beady eyes peeking over the edge of the dashboard.

"That Loverboy?" the injured goblin asked, a slight shake in his voice.

"Yeah," Max added with a grin, "he works for us now. I'm sure he could still pull a few mob strings to make your life take a nosedive, though. You know, *before* the mob finds out he's a snitch."

It was a risky play by my partner, and I watched the mobgoblin's face to see if it would work.

His teeth clenched.

"Well, I ain't a snitch. Find your turncoat on yer own, cops."

"Sorry you see it that way," Max said as he flew past the guy's head and gave it a slap before flying off.

"Are goblins always this tight-lipped?" I asked my partner, trying to keep up.

"No," Max said. "Something's got them scared. Someone."

An NYPD patrol car pulled up.

"Shit," I rasped.

"Don't worry about it. It's Beat."

I recognized her immediately. She was the cop who helped us cross the river to Brooklyn, back during the Blood Claws case. She had cast a wind spell back then, too. It sent our little dingy boat across the water in seconds.

I nodded and she nodded back, obviously recognizing me, too.

"You two get what you want?" she asked Max. "You have about two minutes before the rest of my team shows up."

"But, Beat, *we're* yer team," Max teased.

If I didn't know any better, I'd say that he had a crush on her. She was pretty, but she didn't seem like his type. Too big, for one thing. She was my size.

"Bite me," Beat said, as she walked away. She started pushing the crowd back.

"Last time I tried, you smacked me."

"Can you…" I started.

"What?" Max asked, squinting at me.

"Can you just *not* do that?" I finished, feeling like I'd just bitten into a sour kiwi.

"Do what?"

"The flirting, Max. For the love of…" I gagged. "Please."

"Hey," he countered. "A man's got needs!"

"Not something I want to know, Shakespeare."

Max glared at me and pointed. "Get Loverboy back to HQ. We need to find out where they took my goblin before they off him."

"Max," I argued, "this isn't about Jonny. We have to find the claw. We can't waste anymore time on chasing your fence."

I felt bad for suggesting it, but now that we'd lost him, he was probably out of our reach. We had to find a more direct route to the claw than one snitch goblin.

"Classy idea, Black," he said. "You think maybe yer gettin' jaded a little early?"

"Max…"

"We find Jonny. Period. Get Loverboy to HQ. Now."

He flew off into the night sky.

I got into Junker and sighed.

"How was yer day, sweety?" Loverboy asked me.

I gave him a look to kill.

CHAPTER 27

The interrogation did not go well.

Loverboy was annoying, but he was also pretty damn tough when it came down to it. He wouldn't talk about Jonny. He wouldn't give an inch on the Blood Claw. He didn't give us anything on the new mob boss, who we'd been trying to identify since Mike was catnapped.

"I could beat it out of him," Max muttered into his coffee mug. We sat in the PPD lunchroom, which looked like every other lunchroom you've ever seen. Too small, with not enough tables, and a filthy fridge filled with old food.

"You kind of tried that," I noted, feeling the warmth of my coffee cup on my palms.

"Yer gonna talk smack now? Fine. Give me the rundown."

He did this every once in awhile. We'd only been partners for a few weeks, but he'd probably asked me to give him the rundown a few dozen times.

"Our target has the missing Blood Claw. That could be a wizard. It could be the mob. Either way, it could be used to create an army of tiger-y goblins. We don't want that because we'll fall even further behind the chaos that a new mob boss is causing in New York City."

Max nodded his head, and opened his mouth like he wanted to say something.

"What?" I asked.

"Nuthin', keep goin'."

"No, I want to know what you were going to say."

"You haven't gotten to this part yet, but it's just somethin' that's been buggin' me. The Hunter works for anyone who'll pay enough. Best we can tell, at least. His victims are all over the map, from corrupt politicians to little old ladies walking their dogs." He let out a long breath. "This is the first time he's killed two of the same kind in a row."

"Is that right, Sue?" I asked, projecting my voice to the AI, who was always listening in.

"First off, it ain't yer place to question yer superiors, toots," Sue said in his craggily voice through the room's comm speaker.

"I just ordered some powerful magnets online, jerkoff," I said to the speaker. "Should be here in a day or two. I hear they can take out a server from a mile away."

"Secondly," Sue's voice turned a little warmer, "Shakespeare is right. The Hunter has always avoided a pattern."

"So maybe this is personal?" I asked. "Why would he not like wizards?"

"The better question is why *would* he like wizards?" Sue asked. "Why would anyone?"

"Okay, you're not needed anymore, AIs-hole," I snarked.

Max laughed at my pun and gave the speaker a guilty look. "Thanks, Sue."

Some grumbling was followed by the click of the speaker as Sue dropped back into listen mode.

"Keep goin'," Max said, leaning back in his custom chair on the kitchen counter.

I took a sip of coffee.

"So, we've got one dead wizard, killed in his apartment. He was probably the one who escaped from the Blood Claw ritual back when we saved Mike's ass. The guy who killed the wizard was The Hunter."

Max nodded.

"Another dead wizard, killed in the museum. Howie Sunderland. Also offed by The Hunter. This time we had some mobgoblin company. Why? I have no idea. Maybe they wanted to help clean up. Maybe the wizard was rogue and they wanted to grab the claw from him. Maybe they're cleaning up after themselves. Getting rid of wizards who know about the Blood Claw plans."

"Good," Max said, sounding like a dad listening to his daughter recite the Gettysburg Address well.

It made me feel good. I'm not ashamed to say it, except that's a lie and I'm 100% ashamed to say it. It irked me that I wanted his approval. I shook off the feeling and focused.

"We have one missing goblin," I continued. "A snitch. Your favorite."

Max sneered. “Can’t stand the punk.”

“He just disappeared from a car. Presumed dead.”

“Better not be, or I’ll kill him.”

I nodded. “The mobgoblin we have in custody seems to be a senior mob soldier, but he won’t talk. We have no leverage to make him talk except booting him back to the Netherworld. Meanwhile, Mike is too terrified to leave his damn room, and he won’t know a moment of peace until the mob is gone.”

Max’s eyebrows shot up. “Where the hell did that come from?”

“I spoke with him earlier,” I admitted with a sigh. “He’s a mess, and I don’t blame him. He’ll be a target until the mob is dismantled.”

“The mob is not gonna be dismantled, rookie.”

“Why not?”

He laughed. “Why would you want to dismantle City Hall?”

“I don’t want to…” My brain was having trouble comprehending his question. “Huh?”

“Why would you want to dismantle the NYPD or the PPD?”

“I’m not talking about doing that.” I shook my head. “What the fuck are you talking about?”

“You’re missing the big picture, Black,” Max replied. “The mob is as much a part of this town as the sidewalk. Take away the mob and all you’ve got is the sewers to walk in.”

“Sounds like some old school thinking to me,” I said, defensively.

I had no idea what I was talking about but I wasn't about to admit that to him.

He just shrugged. "We'll find a way to keep your boyfriend safe."

Max knew full well that Mike wasn't my boyfriend, but I didn't bother to go for the bait. I was restless. I wanted to get out of there as soon as possible. All this sitting around and thinking and talking was a waste of precious time.

But the fact was, I didn't know what to do. My gut told me to stick with Max.

Do what he told me to do.

Don't make waves.

Pride will kill you.

I guess my restlessness showed.

"You look like a pressure cooker," Fay said to me as she entered the lounge.

"Nice to see you, too, Fay," I said, with a bit of a snarl.

She shrugged and walked to the coffee machine and filled it up with one of her water spells. She swore that her spell water was tastier than normal water. When she'd asked me to try it out, I passed. I don't like the idea of swallowing water that comes from Fay's palms, thank you very much.

"You okay, Fay?" I asked, realizing that I was taking my angst out unfairly on her.

"Hmmm? Oh. Yeah. Fine. It's just my…" she glanced at Max and clammed up.

"Yer what?" Max asked?

"Nothing, sir."

"Is this one of those woman problem type of things?"

he asked, adjusting his little jacket and straightening his tie. "Cuz I can help you with that."

I wrinkled my nose and Fay sighed heavily.

"It's my mother," she admitted, finally.

"I think I hear Sarge callin' me," Max lied, obviously realizing that it wasn't the kind of problem he'd hoped for. "Be right there, Sarge!"

He flew out the door and, from the yelping sounds, he must have smacked into someone pretty hard.

"What, uh, what about her?" I asked Fay, trying to ignore the awkward moment.

She dropped into the chair across from me and leaned on her elbows. Her eyes were sallow and dry, as if she'd been sleeping and crying at the same time.

"She's trying really hard to get back into my life."

"She *is* your mom," I said. Fay shot me a look. "Isn't that what they're supposed to do?"

"Bethany, she wants to know more about my job. She wants to interfere. Just like she always does."

A little alarm went off in my head. I didn't like the sound of that.

"What does she want to know about?"

"After she told me about the Blood Claws spell, she just got into one of her pushy moods. She even went to Sarge to ask how I'm doing!"

"Oooh. Sorry, Fay."

I wanted to be supportive, but I also wanted to know how curious her mom was, exactly. She'd shared some important info with her daughter that helped us save Mike from the Blood Claws spell. And now she was giving us even more information, but was there an agenda behind helping her daughter?

"She wants to know more about the Blood Claw?" I asked.

"Who knows?" Fay answered, putting her hands up. "Blood Claws. PPD politics. My love life…or lack of one." She let out a long breath. "She's digging everywhere. Makes me feel like I'm back in school."

Fay leaned back and took a sip of coffee, but it came out too fast, and she spilled half her cup on her uniform.

Poor Fay.

She just sat there and stared at the wall while I grabbed some paper towels and wiped her dry.

"Thanks," she finally said after a long silence. "Bethany?"

"Yeah?"

"I don't think I'm ready to be a PPD officer."

I didn't get a chance to argue because she jumped up and bolted from the room.

"I've got something," Graham said over our connection.

"Yeah? What is it?"

"Our second dead wizard. He's one of five owners of the Jersey bar."

"Who are the others?" Max asked, breaking in.

"Some more wizards," Graham replied, *"and Granny G."*

CHAPTER 28

Graham, Bob, and Lou joined me in Max's car.

"I can't believe we gotta hit that old broad up for a lead again," Max complained as he steered around a car that dared to only go ten miles over the speed limit.

"I can't believe we have to visit her for a second time in one year," Bob muttered.

Lou was Granny G's favorite for what that was worth. Last time I saw her she was ready to skewer both of her grandsons, favorite or not.

When we pulled up to her apartment, the lights in her apartment were off.

"Damn it," Max said.

He hit the steering wheel and leaned back in his seat to think. He poured some sunflower seeds into his mouth. It was his way to stop smoking.

He'd tried to stop four times since I met him the month before.

"Maybe she's got company up there," Lou said.

"I'm tryin' to eat here!" Max yelled.

"I'm just sayin'! She likes her slippy time."

Max spit out the sunflower seeds and threw them out the window. A cold rush of air froze us back into silence.

"Call her," I said to Bob.

"What do you mean?"

"I mean call her, Bob. She has a cell phone, remember?" It was hard to forget her cell phone. The gunshot ring tone almost gave all of us a heart attack last time we'd visited her.

"What do you mean?" Bob asked again. He was playing stupid. Nothing scared him more than his grandma.

"I'll do it," Lou said.

"Since when did you get a cell phone?" Bob asked as Lou stuck his nose in his screen to see the buttons better.

"Since Sarge made us deputies. Says we may need it to contact NYPD one day."

"He didn't give me a cell phone!"

"I thought cell phones were a no-no in the PPD?" I asked Max.

"New PPD issue," he replied. "Can't be traced or something. I don't know, Black."

Lou shrugged and put his ear to the phone. "It's ringing."

Max grabbed the phone and put it on speaker.

"You've reached Granny G. Not here right now. Probably in the middle of a big hug. Leave a message."

Beeeep.

"Granny G! This is Lou. I got a cell phone, granny! Anyway, so I need to talk to you, so call me at this number, okay? Bob says, 'Hi!' Say 'hi,' Bob!"

"You just told her I said 'Hi,' so why should I say 'hi' again, you idiot?"

"Say 'Hi' to Granny G, Bob!"

"Fuckin' A, Lou! 'HI, GRANNY!'"

Max ended the call and Bob smacked Lou on the back of the head.

"We need to find her now," I said. "What does she mean she's in the middle of a big hug?"

"No idea," Bob said, fuming.

"I mean I *know*, but I think there might be more to the 'big hug' thing than just...well, you know."

"Wait, what?" Graham asked me. I forgot that he wouldn't have heard the outgoing message.

"Granny G said she was in the middle of a big hug," I said.

"No she did not," Graham said. His eyes went wide. Then he started to go a little pale.

"Jeez, Graham, what the fuck's wrong?" I asked. "You all right?"

"Yeah, just..." he swallowed and tried to compose himself, but he still looked sick. "It's just that her business partners...the ones that own the bar with her—"

"Spit it out, kid!" Max yelled.

"Their names are George Big and Howie Hug."

CHAPTER 29

We heard Granny G before we found her. Which is to say, we found her by *hearing* her before we actually laid eyes on her.

Okay, fine, what I really mean to say is that she makes a lot of noise when she's in the middle of a big hug, okay?

Apparently, I was the bravest one because I was out in front of our little crew as we approached the condo building. The residence of Howie Hug, middle-of-the-road wizard with a thing for booze and old lady goblins, from the sounds of it.

The noises of passion, which ranged from glee to agony, dropped from a set of tenth-story windows like little bombs of nausea.

After a particularly violent bellow, Bob backed away, shaking his head so hard that his nose waved back and forth through the cold winter air.

"I ain't goin' in there, no way," he whispered, as if Granny G could hear him from the tenth floor, while being thoroughly Big Hugged.

"You're going," Max said, shoving him back up onto the sidewalk.

We were pretty much the only ones dumb enough to be walking around the frigid streets. But if Granny G could tell us why her business partner would be on The Hunter's list, then maybe we'd be closer to finding the claw.

She was about to get company.

I just hoped and prayed she'd be pissed about that, and not turned on by the idea.

The doorman had his face in his hands when we walked into the lobby. The sounds of agony and ecstasy bounced off the marble floors. His sweaty face was pale and his eyes were surrounded by bags.

"Can I help you?" he asked.

A male wail filled the room.

"Sorry about that," the doorman said, on the verge of tears. "I've been gettin' yelled at all night, as if I can do anything about it. The police won't even help anymore."

"That's why we're here," I said, flashing my PPD badge quick enough to convince him.

"Yeah?" he asked.

His face got some color back. He was ready to believe anything.

"Yeah," Lou said, a little too enthusiastically. Max shoved his elbow into his ribs. "Ow!"

"Room number, please?" I asked, sticking to business.

"1009." He buzzed the security door open for us and smiled. "Good luck!"

Once we got on the elevator, Lou started laughing.

"That was brilliant! Wasn't that brilliant, Shakespeare?

What do you think of our Bethany now, huh? Fast thinker, this one is. Fast! Great job, BB!"

He slapped me on the shoulder and I tried not to smile. It *was* a good move, but I had to show humility around Max, or I'd pay for it later.

"I got lucky," I said with a shrug.

My partner glanced over to see if I was riding him. I had my poker face on. Hopefully it was enough.

The elevator doors opened and all of us, except Graham, covered our ears. Whatever they were doing to each other sounded like it could do permanent damage.

Something big and heavy hit the front door and shook the doorbell. As we adjusted to the noise, I noticed that no one was actually leaving the elevator.

I sighed and led them out.

I got to the door and was about to ring the doorbell, when the heavy thing hit the door again. I flinched. The thing slid down the door.

And moaned.

"Hello?" I said, putting my ear up to the heavy door.

"Jesus, they're really going at it in there," Bob mumbled.

I looked down.

The hall's carpet was steeped in blood.

CHAPTER 30

Graham pulled his pistol and aimed it at the door handle.

Max slapped his hand down.

"Someone's on the other side of that door, rookie. You want to shoot him in the head to get things started?"

"Sorry, sir," Graham said as he stepped back.

"You two," Max said, pointing to Bob and Lou, "break down the door."

"Us?" Bob choked. "Why us?"

"Yer the strongest. Get goin'."

Bob and Lou looked at each other and rolled up their sleeves.

"Well, all right, then," Lou said.

"More like it," Bob added, his voice a couple of octaves lower. "A little respect. About time." The two goblins lined up, side-by-side. "On 3, then. 1, 2, 3!"

They ran at the door full-speed, shoulders first, in perfect synchronicity. They got rejected by the door, falling to the bloody floor while screaming in perfect synchronicity.

"Yeah, figured," Max said. "Bolted." The pixie flew to the door. "PPD! We're comin' in! Drop yer weapons or the first bullet goes up yer ass!"

"You asshole! You knew that door was too tough to break down!" Bob yelled.

"I suspected, yeah," Max muttered as he tapped on the apartment door. "Now we have to do this the hard way. We're comin' in!" He turned to me. "Cover yer eyes, people."

Max lifted his pistol and shot at the door's hinges. One by one they snapped off the frame. I closed my eyes just in time to cover my eyes from the wood and steel splinters.

"Help me here!" he yelled and I jumped over my goblin bodyguards and hit the door with him. It gave a little bit, cracking under the strain. Graham joined in and the door fell to the apartment floor.

A man's hand stuck out from under the shredded wood panels. I lifted the door up and pushed it aside.

He was dead.

No mistaking that.

One eye was wide open. The other one was split wide open.

By a knife.

"Hunter!" I yelled.

Everyone knew what that meant and dutifully kissed the floor. Everyone but Graham, who had no idea what my warning meant.

A knife landed in his shoulder, knocking him on his back. Max and I covered his body with ours, guns drawn.

Okay, to be precise, I covered his body and Max covered a foot.

Again, The Hunter made like a shadow. The apartment was huge. The large windows were covered in shades, letting just enough light in to spot the killer's dark form.

He was as still as a mannequin.

"Stay right there!" I yelled, moving up to a kneeling position. "Do not move!"

He didn't. He was so still that I wondered if it actually *was* a mannequin.

Then he laughed. It was a soft laugh. I don't think he meant to.

"What's funny, asshole?"

Instead of answering, he slipped into the shadows. I almost fired but spared the refrigerator he'd been standing in front of a split second ago.

I felt Max zip past my ear. A flicking sound behind me made me turn fast and growl.

"Whoa," Lou said, holding up his hands. "Just tryin' to turn some lights on, BB. He must have cut 'em."

I turned back to the dark room. I didn't feel like getting stabbed again.

"You stay here," I told them.

"No way," Bob said.

"Do I have to remind you that this is my job, Bob?"

"Sure, I can always use a reminder, I guess. Old brain and all. Look, I don't want to get in an argument, Bethany."

"Good, then shut your piehole, and stay with Graham."

I flicked on my pen light and cradled it next to my 6er so I could see where I was going. I hugged the walls, crouching and making sure I identified all the possible hiding places.

There was a long, thin hallway straight ahead of me. The dancing light of flame outlined a door from the other side. It was ever so slightly cracked open.

Something passed in front of the flame.

Someone was in that room.

My heart felt like it would do a jig out of my nose. I took a deep breath and calmed myself. It was hard to do when my body kept waiting for a blade to fly from the blackness and lodge into my flesh. But I managed to take a step, and I walked down the hall. I passed by four doors, two on each side of the hall. They were closed. That made me let my guard down.

I heard the whirring noise too late. An arm broke through the door, shattering it into pieces, and a hand grabbed me by the neck. I was lifted off the floor as my nose filled with a smell that was getting all too familiar.

Oil.

I clutched The Hunter's forearms. They were solid as steel. In fact, they *were* steel. My legs dangled and I struggled to catch my breath.

"Shave and a hair cut," The Hunter said.

I could hear the smile in his voice as my eyes adjusted to being able to see him.

The first thing I noticed was that he was a big fucker. The second thing was that his head was covered in a black helmet. It covered his face, too. Its dull black paint looked like some kind of polymer. There was no place for his eyes to see, or his nose to breathe or his mouth to punch.

His face was a solid slate of slight curves, sculpted to barely accommodate the features underneath.

I had a thousand quips to shoot at his ugly ass, but I was too busy choking.

So, I changed.

Full Tiger.

Fast, too. Probably the fastest I've ever done it.

His grip loosened as my neck grew and I dropped to my back paws. My front paws landed on his shoulders, claws drawn. I let gravity do most of the work and shoved him onto the floor. He hit the tile hard and I heard the breath leave his lungs.

Then I roared in his face.

But I'd meant to say, "...Two bits, bitch."

CHAPTER 31

My victory lasted three seconds.

The electric shock froze my body. All I could do was fall to my side as my muscles contracted. I tried to catch my breath but my lungs were trying to remember how to work. I saw The Hunter crawl away and get to his feet.

Then Max knocked him down with two well-placed shoes in the neck.

Max aimed his pistol at the jerk's face but The Hunter rolled out of the way. He pulled out a knife from his belt in one smooth movement and threw it at my partner. The blade clipped his wings. Max twirled mid-air as he tried to stay afloat. But it was no good. He fell to the carpet and his gun popped from his grip.

He scrambled to retrieve the weapon but The Hunter stepped on it.

That's when the air flew into my lungs in one delightful moment. My blood recharged. My brain focused.

The Hunter kicked me in the head.

Progress lost.

I heard him scrambling with someone. Officer Graham, maybe? It was hard to see through the lights dancing around my vision.

A gunshot made me growl.

I wasn't hit. That much I could tell. As I got my vision back, I saw The Hunter standing over someone.

It was Bob.

The Hunter held his arm as if it was wounded. The blood dripping off of his dangling hand verified it was. Bob had used Max's tiny pistol to shoot the most feared criminal in New York.

Nice job, bodyguard.

The Hunter kicked the pistol from the goblin's hand and unsheathed another blade.

I pounced on his back and bit down on the spot where his helmet met his neck. I lucked out and got a fangful of flesh. The Hunter screamed and, with an incredible amount of strength, tossed me over his shoulder.

I landed on Bob.

He shrieked and struggled underneath me. I jumped after the killer as he ran back through the door he'd broken down.

The bedroom was freezing. An open window was letting the winter in. I changed back to human form out of instinct. My cat form just hates the cold that much.

I stumbled across the room and looked down to the street below.

The Hunter was dragging a body into a black van. A

streak of blood ran over the dirty snow on the curb. He looked up at me and gave me a salute.

I reached for my gun and aimed at a rear tire. I rolled off four shots as the vehicle screeched off. It turned the corner, out of sight.

So The Hunter had help. The driver of the van could probably tell us a thing or two.

"Sue, we need—"

"You are fucking kidding me," the AI interrupted.

"We're stopping criminals out here!"

"No. You're not. That's my fucking point!"

"We need a medic and Bloods. You sending them, or not? We need to preserve a crime scene on the corner of 11th Avenue and 30th St. We have tire marks in the snow for a getaway vehicle. At least until..."

A cabbie pulled into the spot where the van had been.

"Now we just need Dick and Pat, dammit."

I closed our connection and ran out of the room. Bob was still on the ground, but he looked okay. He stared at the ceiling. When I stepped into his vision, he blinked.

"Thanks, BB."

"Thank you. You saved me first." I helped him up. My vision went blurry for a second. I was still recovering from the electric shock and the blow to the head. "Where's Max?"

"No idea."

"Shakespeare, you okay?"

"Nothing that Pat can't fix," he said. *"But we have a problem."*

"What is it?"

"Granny G," he said. *"Looks like she bit it."*

CHAPTER 32

It took a full minute to find the right room.

The apartment was huge. I ran around several corners and through a dining room, a den, two bathrooms, and a kitchen.

"Why are we running?" Bob yelled from behind me.

"Max is with your grandma. We need to help him out." I didn't want to tell him the news.

"Is she okay?"

"Where are you goin'?" Lou called from a small gym.

"Just come with me."

Graham stood outside a room. His body language told me that Max was right. Graham stepped aside as we passed and said, "Sorry, guys."

"Sorry, what…" Lou said before he stopped short. "Granny?"

Max stood over her, his fedora off his head.

"Yeah, sorry boys," Max said. "She was gone when I found her."

The goblins tip-toed up to their grandma as if they didn't want to wake her from her eternal slumber.

I looked away.

It was just too painful.

The room had been trashed, rock star style. Broken glass, clothing all over the place, overturned furniture, and even a shot-out plasma TV. I couldn't tell if this was the struggle against an assassin, or a really animated threesome.

I looked up at Lou, expecting to see him struggling with the moment. But he just appeared confused.

He met my eyes and said, "Uh, guys?"

"Yeah," Max said. "Whatta ya need?"

"She's not dead."

"Whatta ya mean?" Max stepped closer and stood on the pillow next to her head. He knelt and put his hand in front of her nose and mouth. "Nothin'. She's dead, Lou."

"Nah, she's just restin'," Bob said, nodding his head.

The first thing I thought was the two of them must have been overcome with grief and denying what their own eyes were seeing.

But then I noticed that Bob seemed kind of disappointed. As if he wouldn't have minded at all if Granny G wasn't around to taunt him anymore.

"You two are—"

"Wait," I said, interrupting my partner who did not like to be shut down like that. He burned a frown into my soul. "She looks dead, guys. What's up? Don't leave us hanging."

They glanced at each other as if they were about to reveal a big secret.

It was Lou who finally spoke up. "You know how human guys kinda, I dunno, drift off after they shine the bone throne?"

"Excuse me?"

"You know. Shoot the fruit."

"Yeah, plow the frau."

"Wait, what are you guys sayin'?" Max asked.

"Scrub the nub. Split the bit."

"Not that! I mean—"

"Press the dress. Hitchhike the deep dike."

"Okay, guys, I get it."

"Plum the annual income."

"OKAY! YES! WE KNOW!" Max yelled, louder than I'd ever heard him yell before.

"Well, that's what goblin women do," Bob said, looking at his feet.

"They fall asleep?" I asked, feeling confused.

"More like they fall into a coma."

Max looked back down at the very dead-looking Granny G.

"She's fuckin' dead," he rasped. "No breath. Irises don't move."

"She's really not," Bob said.

"Watch," Lou said as he knelt beside Granny G's body. "You were amazin'," he whispered

We all made a face, including Lou.

Granny G miraculously turned onto her side and muttered, "Yuh, uh-uh, ya bet, love you too."

"Holy shit," Max said, nearly falling over.

"No, *yer* hot shit, dear," Granny G said, still dead-looking, except now her eyes were closed, and drool dripped from her lips onto the pillow.

"Then we might have a witness here," Max noted, his eyes blinking like mad. "Wake her ass up."

"Female goblins don't wake up," Bob said with a smirk.

"Not until they're good an' ready," Lou added.

"Then get her good an' ready," Max demanded. He glanced around the room. "Where's the other wizard? I thought there were two."

I swallowed. "The Hunter took his body."

"How do you know that?"

"I watched him stuff it into a van before he drove off."

The look on Max's face was cold and threatening.

"You let The Hunter escape?"

"Well, where the hell were you?" I argued back.

"Wait," he said, looking away. "You were down. My wings were injured and he was standing on my gun." He turned his eyes back to mine. "I went to get Graham for help and found him here. Shit." He pointed at me. "Did you get the license plate?"

"No," I admitted with a sigh.

"Dammit, rookie."

"Lay off, Shakespeare," I barked back at him, ready to find his little wings and shove them up his ass. "I did everything I could."

"Guess that isn't enough, then," he challenged, probably hoping I'd dare to even try to shove those wings up his ass.

I wanted to tear into him, but I let it go. He was venting. I was venting. It was how things went. I needed to get used to it. Maybe one day it wouldn't affect me.

If our partnership lasted.

"She's not waking up anymore," Bob said as he stepped back from the bed.

"Then we're bringing her with us," Max declared. "We need to know what happened here. Graham, pick 'er up."

Graham bent over the old goblin and scooped his hands under her. She wrapped her arms around his shoulders and nuzzled her nose into the crook of his neck.

"So big 'n powerful," she muttered, staying in deep sleep.

I'd forgotten how Granny G had taken a liking to Graham when we all met. Apparently, she'd taken a bigger liking than I'd thought. Something about him made her blink her eyes open for a few seconds at a time.

"Granny G," Max ventured, "what happened here?"

"Mmm? Who're you?" Her crossed eyes appeared to be trying to make sense out of Max's face. "Go 'way. Want m'man here to squeeze the knees."

"What is wrong with you people?" Max asked with a sour face. "We got two dead wizards here, lady. You're our only witness."

That seemed to wake her up a little bit, but not much.

"Big and Hug dead?"

Her head drooped again.

"Yeah, they're dead. What can you tell us about it?"

"What a way to go," she said.

Her head fell back and her mouth opened wide. She released a thick and hearty snore.

CHAPTER 33

I helped Graham get Granny G into Max's car. Her head rolled all around as we got her settled. Graham slipped in next to her and I hopped in the front seat.

She was moving in and out of consciousness.

"LADY HURT!" I heard a voice scream from behind me.

I turned quickly and held out my hands. I knew what was going to happen next. I'd seen it twice in the last 24 hours.

"Stop!" I yelled. Dick, the medic, stopped on his heels, about three feet away from me. He peeked over my shoulder to get a better look at Granny G. "Dick. She's just recovering from…"

"GOBLIN SEX!"

A smile cracked his face.

"Yeah," I said, impressed with his ability to spot health issues. We needed a little bit of anonymity, though, being in the middle of Manhattan and all. "Could you keep it down, please, big guy?"

"SURE! HEY PAT! GOBLIN SEX!"

"You officers need us, or not?" Pat asked. Her hands were on her hips and she looked pissed off.

"Max's wings got clipped," I said, pointing my thumb at my partner. "And Graham pulled a blade from his shoulder."

"Let me see, Shakespeare," Pat said as she gestured for him to turn around.

"Be gentle this time, toots," Max said.

Pat knelt down and took a close look at his wings. She reached into her supplies and pulled out a cream.

"We don't have time to mess around," I said.

Max gave me a look to melt the ice. "You mind? I'm getting a rubdown here."

"Really professional of you, partner."

"Oh, I'm getting judged on my professionalism now by the rookie who let The Hunter escape."

"Only after you did the same thing when he tagged me in the thigh."

"The ass," Max said. "Douché."

"I think you mean touché," I corrected.

"No, I'm pretty sure I meant douché, douché."

I could have slapped the jackass, or run away from him. I decided to slip in next to Graham in the back of the car and slam the door shut. I didn't want to share the same air with my partner at the moment.

I glanced over at Graham. He looked at me and tried to smile, but failed.

"Tough partner," Graham said.

Great.

Small talk.

Just what I was in the mood for.

"Yeah," I agreed, finally. "He is. You want him?"

Graham's expression got weird. He looked away as if he was keeping a secret. When he looked out of his window, I recognized that this was how he avoided conversations he didn't want to have. If he couldn't see your lips then he couldn't talk about uncomfortable things.

I tapped him on the shoulder.

"What is it?" I asked.

"Nothing."

"Why are you acting weird?"

"Maybe because I have an oversexed grandma goblin leaning on me?"

"No, you went silent when I asked if you wanted Max as a partner."

He rolled his eyes, but I noticed that he couldn't meet my stare.

Again.

"Look," he said, "I asked Sarge if I could be first in line if you backed out, okay? It's not a big deal."

"Wait, what?" I almost laughed. "You *want* to be Max's partner?" My jaw was fighting to touch the floor. "You know the way he treats people, and you actually want to spend all day with him, day in and day out, all week long, for years?"

"Yeah," he answered, clearly not hearing the heavily inflected sarcasm in my voice. It should have been obvious from the look I was giving him, but apparently not. "Max Shakespeare is the best officer the PPD has ever had. New York or otherwise."

"That's laying it on thick," I said. "He's good, but that doesn't make him a good partner. And being a good partner is also part of being a good officer."

"Hmmm."

"What, hmmm?"

"Nothing. It's just that that's what Max told me about you."

"He said I'm a good officer?"

"No," he replied a little too quickly. "Well, yeah. I guess. Kind of. He said that you'd make a good officer when you knew how to be a good partner."

What the fuck?

That's all I remember thinking.

All the hard work I'd put into swallowing my pride, going along with his moods, and stupid ideas, and he still thought I was a bad partner?

"What do you think?" I asked, digging for a little positive reinforcement. "Am I a bad partner?"

"No, you're not a bad partner," Graham answered seriously. "And I don't think that's what he meant. I think he just has high standards." He looked away again. "Everyone knows you're working hard. Very hard."

"Very hard," Granny G purred. She then smiled and put a hand on Graham's thigh. "So very, very hard, and firm."

Then her eyes fluttered open.

CHAPTER 34

Granny G smacked her lips a few times and wiped the drool off her chin before looking up at Graham.

"I don't remember you being there, handsome. How was I?"

"I…I…uh…"

She didn't wait for him to answer. She spotted me staring.

"Oh," she said with a grunt, "it's you."

"Hi, Granny G."

Her frown softened for a split second.

"Are Big and Hug dead?" she asked in a groggy, half-conscious voice.

"Yeah."

"Fuck. What a loss. Good, big-boned lads gone to waste." She nodded off again.

I glanced out the window at Max. He caught me staring and held up a finger as if to say "one minute." I nodded. We'd have to mend things up before we figure out what our next step was.

Granny G took in a deep breath as if waking up from a scary dream.

"Who did it?" she asked, but her eyes kept fluttering shut.

Max would not like me sharing information with a goblin. I didn't trust her. Nothing in my gut told me it was a good idea to tell her anything.

But, for some reason, I said, "The Hunter."

The old goblin gasped and then tried to cover it up with a fake cough.

"He didn't want you dead," Graham said, trying to comfort her. "Right, Black? I mean, I heard The Hunter doesn't miss."

"Did they say anything, Granny?" I asked.

"The wizards? Like what?"

"Like about the Blood Claw."

She pursed her lips. "Yeah. Yeah, that's right. The two of 'em were goin' on about a bloody claw, whatever that is. I thought maybe it was a new position." Her eyelids got heavy again. "Those boys were always lookin' for new ways to..."

She nodded off.

"I don't think I needed to hear that," I said.

I took a deep breath and closed my eyes. I had to think, but Max tapped on the car window and gestured for me to join him outside.

"If she wakes up again, ask her if she saw what happened to the wizards."

"You got it."

The chill wind slapped my face as I stepped out of the car.

"She okay?" Max asked.

"Yeah, she keeps waking up and nodding off. She says the wizards mentioned something about the Blood Claw, but I haven't gotten any further."

"Good, okay." He paused, his mouth open. "Look, Black, I didn't mean to lay it on so heavy about The Hunter."

Dammit. He was apologizing for the first time ever and all I could think about was my brain burp in the car with Granny G.

"…he's dangerous, and I should have been there to…"

What should I do? Should I tell him I'd told her about The Hunter?

"…want to stick my gun up his…"

No. He didn't need to know. But he'd probably find out anyway. What the hell was I thinking? Of course I wouldn't tell him.

"I told Granny G that The Hunter killed them," I blurted.

Then, as if I was somehow disassociated from myself, I swear I felt my brain roll its 'eyes' and drone, 'Way to go, mouth.'

Max stopped mid-apology, his mouth frozen in place. After a few seconds, he closed it. Then he closed his eyes.

He turned to fly away, and screamed, "OUCH!" because he'd forgotten about his injured wings.

Instead, he walked around the front of the car.

"Sorry," I called after him.

He just raised his hand and wagged the middle finger at me. He got in the driver's seat and honked the horn.

"Let's go!"

I didn't blame him. I was still prone to run-at-the-mouth syndrome. I needed to get my mouth to slow down and wait for my rookie brain to catch up.

Bob and Lou climbed in the back seat and squeezed in tight. I popped the passenger door open and dropped in like a deflated ball.

The six of us looked miserable.

"What do we do now?" Lou asked, breaking the silence.

"Graham!" Max shouted as he turned to face him.

"Sir?"

"Who's the other owner of the Jersey bar?"

"It's not clear, sir. The fifth owner was listed as an LLC. An investor maybe?"

"What's the name of the LLC?"

"Wizzards. With two z's."

We all looked at each other, knowing full well what the "wizz" meant.

"Didn't know wizards were so fucked up," Bob grumbled.

"*Sue*," I said through the connector.

"Whatta you want now?"

"We need to know the owner of a company called Wizzards, with two z's."

"The owner is Pisstols, LLC with two s's."

"I'm serious, Sue," I grumbled.

"So am I, jerk face."

"Fine, then who owns Pisstols?"

"Tinkle, Tinkle Little Star."

"Stop messing with us, Sue."

"I don't mess."

I looked over at Max who shook his head. "Sue doesn't do the whole joke thing."

"Okay, keep checking for ownership until you find a person's name."

"Could take awhile. I'm seein' 7,894,711 records here."

"Just do it, Sue" Max chimed in.

"Awright, awright, keep yer underoos on, Max."

"New plan," Max said, turning to Bob and Lou. "We wait for your ancestor here to wake up and tell us who the fifth owner is."

"Or..." I started to say until I stopped myself.

Everyone looked at me.

"What, Black?" Max asked.

"Or Lou whispers sweet nothings in her ear. It woke her up a little bit before."

"No way," Lou said. "Yer turn, Bob."

"I ain't doin' it."

"It's yer turn!"

"Screw you," Bob barked, "ya liver-smellin' lobster snatch."

"Really, Bob?" I asked with a wince.

"Sorry! He just pisses me off sometimes."

"I'll do it," Graham said in a low voice, packed with the drama of the moment.

He sighed as if he'd just volunteered to give his life for his country. Then, he leaned into Granny G's ear and whispered.

To this day, I don't know what he said but it damn well worked.

A little too well.

Granny G's eyes popped open and she smushed her face into Graham's face. The poor guy waved his arms around, trying to find something to hold onto so he could break free and grab some oxygen. Bob and Lou both pulled on her thick nightgown but she was too strong for them. It took me and Max to finally yank her free from Graham's lips.

Lips which were now hickied so hard that it looked like he was wearing lipstick.

"Granny," Lou yelled, "settle down! It's me, Lou!"

"I know who you are, you idiot," she snapped back at him. "Now, let me go. I gotta give this hottie a taste of the Granny G spot!"

It took a couple of minutes of restraining her until she started to settle down. We thought we had her under control when she lunged at Graham again. Lou pulled her back down onto the car seat.

"Maybe you oughtta catch a ride with Dick and Pat," Max suggested.

"Get that shoulder wound cleaned out," I added.

Poor Graham's shoulders slumped and he got out of the car.

"Call me," Granny G yelled as the door slammed shut.

"Okay Granny," Max stated. "We need you to focus now. Can you do that?"

"Yer that Shakespeare guy, right?"

"That's me."

She crossed her arms in defiance. "I ain't tellin' you dick."

"If you want us to find who killed Big and Hug, then you need to tell us who the other owners of the bar are."

"The bar? My bar?"

"Yer bar, yeah."

"Sunderland," she said.

Max shook his head. "He's dead, too."

"Yer fuckin' kiddin' me." She was gawking. "The Hunter?"

I felt Max's eyes on me and avoided looking back at all costs.

"Yeah," he said. "The Hunter. So what's it gonna be?"

She looked around the car at each of us and let out a sigh. "I'm a goddamn informant now, ain't I? Twice in a row I help you bozos. If this gets out—"

"It won't, Granny G," Lou assured her.

"Yeah, Granny G," Bob added, nodding his head.

"What the hell do you know?" she said to Bob with a sneer.

The expression on Bob's face made me want to tear her a new one, but I controlled my temper. She must have sensed my hostility, though, because her eyes darted to mine.

I smiled.

She sighed again.

"Dirk Champion," she said, finally. "He lives in Washington Heights."

CHAPTER 35

I thought Max usually drove too fast. In fact, I had gotten in the habit of pointing out old ladies, bicycles and red lights because, well, he didn't seem to have any interest in steering around them.

But after ten blocks of driving, I realized that I had no idea just how fast he could go.

He took a turn onto 13th Street, didn't like what he saw, and went into reverse. When a truck pulled in behind us, he swerved just in time to squeeze his boat of a car onto a sidewalk. An empty sidewalk, as luck would have it.

I genuinely thought someone would die if he didn't dial it back.

"Uh, Max?" I managed to say, even with my guts fighting intense G-forces.

"Zip it, cat. I don't need a backseat driver right now."

He sideswiped a hot dog stand. I looked back in time to see its owner shaking his fist at us.

"Yeah, actually, you do."

"You know how many decades I been drivin' in this city? Never once has anyone been injured that we know about."

"That we know about."

"Yeah. That we know about. Got a problem with that?"

He turned onto the West Side Highway, making all of us lean hard to the left.

I spun to see if the goblins were okay. Their mouths hung open and they made little beeping sounds.

"Goblins don't like speed much," Max announced with a load of glee in his voice.

He cackled just to make it super clear that he was enjoying himself.

We got from 13th Street to 169th Street in five minutes.

I then managed to extract the exact address from Granny G once we pulled off the exit.

Predictably, there was no parking to be found anywhere. The streets uptown are so narrow that he couldn't double park. So Max did the only thing he could do. He pulled up on the sidewalk and cut the engine.

I just shook my head and closed my eyes. What was I supposed to do?

"You guys coming?" I asked Bob and Lou.

They just stared ahead, mouths still wide open.

Max walked off, laughing.

"You can be a real jerk," I yelled after him. I turned back to the goblins. "We'll be upstairs, guys. Don't worry, I'll be fine."

I don't think they heard me.

Just before I got out of the car, Granny G's eyes shut

and she tilted until she was leaning on Lou. She fell asleep again.

"She said 5G, right?" Max asked as he browsed the directory for the buzzer.

He didn't wait for my answer.

He just pressed the button.

No answer.

He took a few steps back onto the sidewalk.

"Take these things off," Max said, pointing to the bandages on his wings.

"That's not a good idea."

"Did I ask yer opinion?"

"No, and yet I gave it. Free will and all that."

"Do it. I'll fly up and scope out the fifth floor."

"No."

I flashed my claws.

"You threatening me, Black?"

I stuck a claw into the door jam and jiggled it in as deep as it would go and then slid it down until I heard a click.

The door popped open.

"Where did you learn that?" he asked, his eyes almost as big as the goblins'.

"There's a lot you don't know about me, partner," I said with a smirk.

We pulled our firearms from their holsters and took the stairs. By the time we'd reached the fifth floor, Max was out of breath.

"Not used to walking much, are you?"

"What makes…you…say that?" he asked between gasps.

"Oh, nothing. Ready?"

He nodded and I pulled the stairwell door open. 5G was directly across the hall.

We approached the door quietly and put our ears to it. It was dead silent.

"Washington!" Max yelled. "Open up! PPD!"

Nothing.

A neighbor poked her face out to see what was going on.

"Please return to your apartment," I said it with as much authority as I could muster. "Official business."

Max had his impressed expression on.

The snooper closed the door slowly.

"You want to try that claw thing again?" Max asked.

I lit up my claws and turned the door handle. It was open.

I smiled down at my partner.

"Yer funny, Black. Keep pushin' my buttons."

He slipped in, pistol up.

The living room was a small space, but the decor was elaborate gold, rich leather, and antiques. Washington had expensive taste.

Max signaled for me to head left, down the hall to the bedroom. He went right, toward the kitchen and den.

That was when my nose picked up on an unwelcome scent. Someone had pissed themselves. Usually a sign of incontinence or death. I knew I wouldn't like what I saw when I leaned into a door way.

But I didn't know it would be that bad.

An old man was splayed across his bed. His limbs were outstretched as if he was greeting death. A slash across his chest was crossed by another cut that went all the way down to his belly.

"Fuck," I whispered.

I needed to keep quiet. The Hunter could still be in the apartment. I took a deep breath and stepped toward the body.

The closet door was slid open and no one was in there. I leaned down to check under the bed. Nothing but stored clothing bins.

I came around the other side of the bed and steeled myself to look at the dead wizard's face.

His eyes were open.

But they weren't still.

He was looking at me.

He blinked.

"Sue! Medic! We have a live one!"

"On it," Sue said.

My tone must have killed his attitude. Or someone had reprogrammed him.

"Help is on the way," I told the man. "Are you Washington?"

He whispered something, but I couldn't hear what. I partially transformed so my ears could hear the message of the dead.

I put my ear to his mouth. He coughed up a little blood, and that cleared his throat enough for him to get out, "Baudelaire. Harlem. Rook takes queen."

He then exhaled his last.

CHAPTER 36

"Max," I said, *"in here."*

"Yer gonna want to see this, Black," he replied.

"Yeah. Same."

"Den."

"Be right there."

I'm not sure why I found it tough to leave the old man there. He was dead. He didn't care, but I felt guilty that he'd be alone.

"Be right back, Washington," I said.

I kept my 6er out. I could smell the oil again. It was different this time though. It was a burnt smell.

"I smell oil, Max," I said out loud.

"We're clear, Black. Just get in here."

I made a mental note that I should always do a partial before stepping into danger. It would be exhausting if I did it too much, but my human brain was getting better at interpreting the tiger senses that flooded in every time I changed.

Max had his pistol back in its harness. He sat on top of a leather chair, his feet dangling over the edge.

"Yer not gonna believe this," he said as he looked down to the Persian rug beneath him.

I saw the feet first. Black boots stuck out.

Black fatigues.

Black gloves.

Armored arms.

And a black polymer mask with creepy curves where the nose and chin were hiding.

"Shit," I said. "You do that?"

"Nope."

The Hunter was laying in his own blood. It was a pool of red that was still working its way slowly through the intricate patterns of the expensive rug.

"I don't see any wounds," I said.

"Turn him over. Must be on the back."

I knelt beside him and nudged on his shoulder. He was heavy.

I almost asked him if we should hold off. Maybe we should wait for the Bloods to show up and do their thing.

Then I remembered Mike.

If Max was okay with me checking out the corpse, then I was okay with it.

I got my feet under me and lifted until the assassin rolled over on his front.

His back was a mess of flesh and blood.

"What the fuck?" Max and I asked at the same time.

"That looks like a wild animal got to him," Max said.

I knelt down and took a closer look at the damage. The edges of the skin were ragged.

Six puncture wounds near the back of the neck looked like a bite. Four slashes down his back had pushed his armor off of his body.

"It was an animal," I said.

"It looks like a tiger."

"A little, yeah. The attack is like a big cat. Puncture wounds in the neck to bring the prey down, four slashes down the torso to bleed him out."

"So a tiger then," Max repeated with more than a little fear in his voice.

"No," I said. "Look at the pattern of the teeth on the back of his neck. That's too small to be a tiger. And the slashes on the back are definitely from claws with those jagged edges. But the claws are too far apart."

"So a small-mouthed, big-clawed tiger."

I shrugged.

We stared at the body for a moment. I hoisted The Hunter back onto his back so the Bloods could have the best approximation of a pure crime scene.

"You want to do it?" Max asked.

I knew what he meant. He didn't have to tell me that the mask needed to come off.

"Curiosity killed the cat," I replied. "*You* do it."

He smirked and hopped down off the chair.

He took a deep breath leaned down, dug his fingers under the chin and pulled.

It didn't budge.

He tried again. Nothing. No movement at all.

"The fuckin' thing is grafted to his skin, from the feel of it."

Against my better judgment, I said, "Let me try."

I gave it all I had, but Max was right. It felt like the mask was attached to a steel wall with a steel bolt. No movement at all.

"Guess we'll just have to wait, then," Max said. "Look at that."

He pointed to the dead man's arms. The thick shirt was filled with holes at the elbow. I poked at one of the holes. The cloth was burned. I held up the ash for Max to inspect.

He smelled it.

"That the same oil you smelled before?"

"Yeah, maybe. But it's burnt."

I slid my fingers into one of the holes, and pulled the cloth apart so we could get a better look at what was underneath.

It was a mechanical joint of some kind. Signs of the shining steel poked through the black burnt surface.

"It's some kind of prosthesis," I said.

"But his arm is underneath."

I found the outlines of the device under his clothes and followed it up to his shoulder, which was protected by armor. I tapped on it, and it made a deep thunk that reminded me of something. I got on all fours and sniffed at it.

Could it be?

"Hey, no eating the leftovers, cat."

"Hilarious. Keep pushing my buttons, partner. It's a battery."

"What's a battery?"

"The shoulders are surrounded by two battery cells. Protected by a rubber skin."

"They power the prosthetics?"

I shrugged. "They power something. Maybe there's tech in that mask of his."

I knocked on that, too. It was solid as a rock. I ran my finger over it, and found out that it was also as smooth as silk.

The mask started to smoke.

The smell of burning metal filled the room.

"Back off!" Max yelled, pulling on my hand.

We took a few steps back and watched the mask melt around The Hunter's face. The smell of flesh joined the potpourri of yuck.

Then the gloves smoked.

Then the boots.

I popped open a window to let some air in.

Max and I climbed out onto the fire escape.

When we stopped coughing, I managed to say, "Did that jerkoff just self-destruct?"

"A pro until the end," Max said, staring at the remnants of The Hunter. "He didn't want anyone to identify him or his methods when he died. Smart. We'll be lucky to get dental ID on him if he did a thorough enough job, which I'm sure he did."

"Shit."

"Yeah. Shit."

"Just to make sure this day gets even worse, I have something to show you, too."

"Washington?"

"What's left of him."

CHAPTER 37

We moved to the next window on the fire escape.

The wizard's dead eyes looked back at us when we peeked into the window.

It was locked. Max pulled out his pistol and I put my hand out.

I took off my jacket and wrapped my elbow in the leather. I stepped up to the window, pulled my arm back, and slammed it against the glass.

It shattered, but it made a blunt noise. A dog barked, but anyone with lesser hearing wouldn't have heard it.

I gave it a couple more hits to clear the jagged pieces, and unlatched the window. I crawled into the bedroom with Max on my tail.

Max stood on the bed and examined the body.

"We're not doing too hot, are we?" he asked, hands on his hips.

"We're trying, but the fucker in the den was damn good. At least that's over."

"Is it?" Max asked.

He knelt down and poked at the body. He pulled out a handkerchief from his overcoat, and cleaned off a small area of the vertical wound.

"Same type of wound," he noted.

"What?" I got in for a closer look.

He was right.

When I saw Washington splayed out on the bed, I'd just assumed that The Hunter had used his knife again.

But the wounds, both the vertical and horizontal, were caused by claws. The same fang marks were on the wizard's neck.

"What the hell is going on?" I asked.

"No idea. You smell anything else?"

"Just the smoke from our self-destructing assassin out there. Everything else is cloaked in that stench." I stood back up and put my hands on my hips. "He wasn't dead when I found him."

"You kiddin' me?" Max asked. "What a way to go. Poor guy."

"He said something." I tried to remember it.

"What was it?"

I clenched my eyes shut and bit my lip. The words were there, but they just weren't coming to me.

"Come on, Black, spit it out," Max complained.

"I'm thinking, Max," I shot back, giving him a look. "For fuck's sake, give me a break, will ya?"

"How about you give the dead guy a break and tell me his dying words."

"Max, I swear to…" I caught myself and took a deep

breath. "Okay, okay, I got it." I pointed at the dead wizard. "He said, 'Baudelaire. Harlem. Rook takes queen.'"

Max went silent.

I enjoyed the moment.

"You know a Baudelaire?" I asked.

"No," Max said, more to himself than me, "but Harlem has a few chess clubs. One of them is a wizard hangout."

The knock on the door was loud enough to wake the whole building.

"You call for backup?" Max asked.

"I called for medics, but I don't think Dick is the kind of guy to knock before he enters."

Max pulled his pistol out of the holster and I followed.

The banging on the door started up again and didn't stop.

"I didn't lock it," I said. *"Did you lock it?"*

"I didn't lock it."

"Maybe it's Bob and Lou," I suggested hopefully.

"They strong enough to shake the whole floor?"

"Good point. It could be the superintendent or maybe the fire department."

"Then we'll give them quite a welcome."

Max stood on one side of the door and I stood on the other. I reached for the handle and Max held up three fingers…

Two fingers…

One finger…

I pulled the door open and aimed at Sir Pickle's face.

He threw his hands up, though his expression didn't change.

I aimed the 6er at the floor and we all shared an awkward moment of silence.

"Sorry, Sir Pickle," I said, letting out a controlled breath. "We're just in a bit of a…uh…well…"

"Pickle?" suggested Max.

"Shut up," I hissed at him.

He giggled.

"Well," Sir Pickle spoke up, "are you going to pursue the path of tradition, rich with the history of natural and supernatural?"

Max and I looked at each other to see if anyone knew what the vampire was talking about.

"Perhaps the welcoming of that which is unwelcome is in order."

"Vampire, talk English fer fuck sake," Max spewed in his best English.

"You need to invite me in, Officer Shakespeare."

CHAPTER 38

The body was smoldering as we stood over it.

I covered my mouth with a napkin I'd snagged from the kitchen.

There was not a threat of fire anymore. The destructive agent was an acid from the looks of it. It left everything charred, melted and smoking, but there wasn't any flame.

"You found him like this?" Sir Pickle asked.

"Approximately," Max said. The vampire glanced at my partner, who couldn't quite meet his stare. "Pretty much."

"I know what approximately is, Officer Shakespeare."

"Yeah?" Max growled back. "Then you know that I'm approximately pissed off that you're on a crime scene without any fuckin' clearance? Maybe you can *approximately* tell me what the hell yer doin' here?"

Sir Pickle looked down on him with a disdain for the ages.

"Approximately," Max repeated, glaring back.

"The highest authority asked me to attend to the consequences of your incompetence."

"Our what?" Max shook his head as if trying to straighten out his brain. "What the hell are you talkin' about, ya bloodsucker?"

"Merely repeating what the one you call Sarge conveyed to me, officer. No need to sunder the little civility left to us in these dark times."

"Do you know what he's talkin' about, Black?"

I shrugged.

"If this is The Hunter, then where are the blades?"

Max and I looked down at the corpse. The melted mess was impossible to sort out, but I realized that Pickle was onto something.

"I didn't see any daggers," I said to Max. "Did you?"

"Who can tell with that ball of jam on the floor?"

"We might have missed them," I admitted.

"This is why you don't touch things before the Bloods arrive," Sir Pickle admonished. "You know better, Officer Shakespeare."

Max's ears turned red. "You know what I know better, ya half teaspoon of hepatitis in a sack of hemoglobin? I know that I've been in the field for decades, while you hid in yer souped up broom closet, talkin' to things in boxes and rubber baggies."

"Guys," I interrupted, before I was interrupted right back.

"Perhaps you meant to say you've been interrupting the natural flow of investigative best practices by inserting your minuscule nose into corners best left to men of my caliber."

"Men? MEN? Yer not a man, ya porcelain-dicked blood bubble."

"Enough!" I yelled. I inserted myself in between the two of them and met Sir Pickle's cold eyes. "Sir Pickle, if you can't tell us why you're here, then can you tell us what you notice?"

He didn't look mad, but I could feel the tension in the room. It didn't take a tiger's senses to know when two guys are reaching their breaking points.

The vampire turned away, as if to collect himself. When he turned back, I sensed his anger had subsided.

"Yes, Bethany Black. What I notice is that the body on the ground fits all eyewitness descriptions of The Hunter. Even in this state, I can tell that he wears the armored mask and body armor from PPD records."

"Good to know. Thank you."

Sir Pickle nodded his head at me and shot Max a look.

"I also notice that there are signs of more than just body armor. I believe the assassin has worn an exoskeleton for decades."

"An exoskeleton?" Max asked, breaking his hissy fit long enough to participate.

"Yes, an exoskeleton. Machinery worn on the body to enhance strength, speed and possibly agility, if the technology works in tandem with a sophisticated form of Artificial Intelligence."

"You mean A. I.?" asked Max.

"Oh, how excellent. Acronyms are an advanced usage of language, Officer Shakespeare." The look on Sir Pickle's face was exquisite. "Color me impressed."

"Fuck you, fang fart," Max said, waving his hand

dismissively. "My point is that The Hunter has been killing for years."

"And your point is?" Sir Pickle asked.

"My point is that what yer talkin' about didn't exist when he started killin', smart guy."

Pickle tilted his head, actually looking impressed this time. "In most circles, no."

The silence in the room asked a thousand follow-up questions.

"So you're saying that The Hunter has had exoskeleton tech for years?" I asked.

"I won't know the answer to that until the Bloods are done with the body, and hand the tech off to me. *If* they choose to do so."

"Why wouldn't they do so?" I asked.

"Don't answer that, bloodsucker," Max barked.

"Hey," I said, turning toward Max. "You're keeping secrets from me now?"

"I'm not keeping secrets from you, rookie," Max replied evenly. "I'm keeping gossip and hearsay from you. The Bloods and the bloodsucker don't see eye to eye."

"They've been hiding evidence about The Hunter from me for years," Sir Pickle muttered.

Max threw his hands in the air."Bullshit!"

"It's one of the reasons I'm here, in fact," the vampire said, looking down his nose.

"Okay, Sir Pickle," I said, "no more games, please. How did you know we're here?"

Sir Pickle looked to be pondering his options, which were somewhere in the hundreds, if the time passed was any indication.

"Sue and I are well acquainted," he finally said.

Max pointed his little finger at Pickle. "Yer hacking again, aren't you?"

"No, he told me freely. I wanted to get here before the Bloods, who are enraged about how busy you're keeping them by the way, so I could, how do you put it, help."

Max crossed his arms. "Uh-huh. Help."

"Yes. Help."

"Help, huh?"

"Help."

I interrupted the useless posturing with a real question that could maybe get us the hell out of that stinking room. "So how can you help, Sir Pickle?"

He glanced at me and then turned to the body. He knelt down and removed a small pouch from his jacket's inside pocket. He delicately untied a string and pulled out a small magnifying glass. He leaned over the body and examined it through the glass, moving his body over the corpse, and running his eyes from head to foot.

It was a little creepy. From the look on Max's face, he agreed with that sentiment.

Sir Pickle focused on a spot near The Hunter's elbow. He scraped some burnt substance, and checked for it under his fingernail.

He stood and approached us, holding out his dirty finger.

"I require enzymes and electrolytes, if you please."

Max and I glanced at each other, confused.

Sir Pickle let out something approximating a sigh. "Would one of you kindly spit on this?"

"I haven't had anyone ask me that for a good two days," Max said with an annoying smirk.

He hocked one up on the vampire's finger.

Sir Pickle took out the glass again and inspected it.

He wiped off his hand and said, "Your next destination is 7866 Broadway." His eyes were calm as he added, "You must hurry."

"The hell with that," Max said. "We have a lead from the stiff in the bedroom. We're headed to Harlem to check on a chess club."

"The Rook Takes Queen?" asked Sir Pickle, his eye twitching slightly.

"Maybe. That's what the dead guy said anyway." Max looked at me. "Right, Black?"

"Yeah. How do you know that name, Sir Pickle?"

"It's the building above a previous location in which I was employed. It's also, in fact, where I was about to insist you attend to."

"So yer sayin' that the dead wizard's dying breath was the name of a chess club that happens to be right above a basement that has somethin' to do with what you just scraped off The Hunter?"

"Precisely."

"That's a series of goddamn coincidences, vampire."

"Isn't it, though?" Sir Pickle deadpanned.

Max let out what could only be called a tiger growl. He turned on his heels and walked out of the apartment.

I smiled at Sir Pickle. His expression didn't change, but he nodded ever so slightly.

"You fuckers comin', or what?" Max yelled from down the hall.

"After you, Officer Black."

"Why thank you, kind sir," I said with a bow.

CHAPTER 39

The goblins had made a full recovery, and were bickering in the backseat when Max and I slipped into the car.

When I looked around for Sir Pickle, he was gone.

"Where did he go?" I asked.

"Who cares? Better keep his nose out of this until I get some time to interrogate him."

"Interrogate him for what?"

"Whatta ya mean, fer what?" He shot back. "How the hell can he look at a chunk of burnt flesh, and tell us to go to exactly the spot where we intended to go, anyway?"

He was right. It *was* odd. But I didn't like the idea of Sir Pickle getting in trouble for helping us.

Max pulled away from the curb at a hundred miles per hour, as usual. I got a glimpse of a PPD vehicle pulling into our spot. I turned to see the silhouettes of the Bloods getting out.

One of them stopped and watched us drive off.

I got a chill.

"What are the Bloods like?"

"Like Hell."

"Why have I never met one at the PPD?"

"They keep a low profile."

Max was keeping it simple. Just like him when he had something to hide.

"You don't want to mess with the Bloods, BB," Lou said.

He gently guided his granny's nodding head onto his shoulder.

""Yeah, they're trouble," Bob added. "Even the mob knows to steer clear of a scene if they're on the job."

"So I've heard. But why? I mean, I've studied the PPD my whole life. And in all the books I read about it, the Bloods get these little mentions that don't amount to anything."

"Tell ya what," Max said. "You shut up about the Bloods, and I'll give you a good and proper introduction after this is all over."

I eyed him. I felt like I was making a deal with the devil that I never asked for in the first place.

Harlem was hopping. The sidewalks were filled with New Yorkers on a Saturday night. Normal people having normal fun. I'd wanted to be a PPD officer my whole life, but right then I would have loved to join them. I was getting tired of goblins and pixies and wizards. And murders. Less murders would have been okay with me.

"There it is," Max said.

I followed his gaze to a small, windowless building. The windows had been bricked over. The front door was a steel thing with a big bouncer beside it. His hands were folded in front of him. The bulge in his jacket meant we had a situation here.

Max double-parked across the street and down the block a little. Just enough so we didn't call attention to ourselves.

"What's the plan?" I asked.

"Good question. Lemme get a lay of the land."

He glanced up at the tops of the buildings and down to the sidewalks and the gutters. He stepped over the car seats and walked across the snoring Granny G to peek out the back window.

He hopped back into the driver's seat and sighed.

"Not much to work with," he said.

Then, ever so slowly, he turned his little head and looked at me. He tipped his fedora back just a bit and scratched his 10 o'clock shadow.

"Why are you looking at me like that, Shakespeare?"

"You play chess?"

"Hell yeah, she plays chess," Bob said, probably remembering all the times I'd beaten him.

Max kept his beady eyes on me. "How good are you? Could you pass for a pro?"

"I'm good, I guess. There's not a lot to do in The Zoo except play games and read. Not pro-level good, though." I then felt a sudden bolt of coldness hit me. "Wait, you don't want me to go in there to play chess with wizards, do you?"

"You got a better idea?"

I looked out the window at the chess club and its menacing bouncer. He might have sensed me because he turned his little head on that thick neck of his and seemed to stare back.

I sunk back down in my seat.

I *wanted* to have a better idea. Something with badges showing and guns blazing and Sarge saying, "The PPD would be nothing without you, Bethany Black."

But all I managed to say was, "No."

CHAPTER 40

"Where's the invite?" the chess club bouncer asked me in a voice so low that I felt it shake my bladder.

Invite. What invite?

Think fast.

"My dog ate it," I said with my best charming smile.

He didn't smile back.

"I'm Bethany. Bethany Black." I held my hand out to shake his but he didn't offer a hand back. "A friend of mine told me he'd meet me here. Maybe I'm on a list?"

"No invite, no entry."

"What's your name?" I asked.

"Endofyer," he said. "Endofyer Evening."

I laughed. That was good. He smirked back. It didn't have a lot of joy in it, but I got the sense that this guy didn't have a lot of joy to give.

"You're funny," I said. "Do you play chess, too?"

"Chess is for wizards." His smirk went away. But he

was still talking to me, so I still had a shot at getting past him.

"I'm a wizard," I lied.

"Congratulations."

"Isn't this a chess club for wizards?"

"Among other things."

"Okay, that's not fair. Now it's all mysterious. I have to get in. Come on, Endofyer. Throw a girl a bone."

He tried to gauge if I was flirting with him. I guess I was. I was out of practice, but I could feel my groove coming on.

"My name is Joe."

"Joe! My dad's name was Joe." Another lie. "Listen, Joe, will you let me in if I show you a trick?"

He studied me for a moment, as if his eyes were a polygraph test. His voice rolled up like an approaching stampede. "Who's the wizard who invited you?" he asked.

I had to think fast and I did. "Dirk Champion."

I know we shouldn't speak ill of the dead, but I was pretty sure that using the name of the dead to lie yourself into a chess club was probably a no-no, too.

Joe's eyes went wide for a second. "Why the fuck didn't you say so?"

"You didn't ask, Joe. So can I go in?"

He didn't budge.

"Show me the magic trick," he said. "Then I'll let you in."

I held up both of my hands. I showed him the back of them and then showed him my palms.

Then I popped my claws.

Sir Pickle had swapped in a set of magical claws to

replace my declawed pads. The weapons cast an intense blue-green glow that was as impressive as the ten long claws that popped out from the tips of my fingers.

Joe managed to let out a small whistle.

"Can I touch one?" he asked, reaching out a beefy finger. I nodded. His flesh touched the tip of my thumb and he pulled his hand back with a big hiss of air. "Fuckin' A, sharp."

He stuck his cut finger in his mouth as he stepped aside and opened the door for me.

"Put in a good word with Mr. Champion for me," Joe said.

"You got it, Joe. Thanks."

The smoky room was lit by salon-style chandeliers and wall sconces of orange glass. A dozen or so tables filled the space with no symmetry. The chess players were all wizards. You can just tell when you see one. It could be braided eyebrows or an extra-large bulge in the jeans or a face tattoo. Wizards just like to broadcast to the edge of your consciousness that they're different.

Bunch of posers, in my opinion.

Taking a look at the boards around me, I recognized a few tactics and realized I was in the presence of some smart posers.

I spotted the bar on the far side of the room and wove my way through the rancid mist of cigars, weed, and vegan-tobacco, non-GMO, gluten-free hibiscus leaves.

If I was going to go through with this stupid plan, then I had to have a drink in me first.

I snagged the bartender's gaze and he took his damn time coming to me. His dreadlocks bounced with every step and the bells woven into his hair made him sound like the arrival of Santa's sled.

"Manhattan," I said, yearning for my favorite drink.

If he mixed it right, maybe it would take the edge off of what I was about to do.

Stupid, stupid idea.

Without a word or a smile, the bartender mixed a half-assed Manhattan. He slid it in front of me, daring me to critique his mixing skills. I was tempted.

I didn't like the guy.

There was something about him.

I took a sip of the weak piss. That drink wouldn't give a bee a buzz.

"You playin', or what?" a scratchy voice asked me from down the bar a ways.

"Sure," I said to the old woman.

Her dreadlocks flowed down her Rastafarian dress that she wore more like a robe. She shuffled past me and sat at an empty table. She took a white queen in one hand and a black queen in the other. She put them behind her back and mixed them up.

I chose the left hand.

White queen.

"Last time you'll win tonight, girl."

"We'll see."

The match wasn't much of a match. She was good. Better than me. My goal wasn't to win. My goal was to get info.

And if that didn't work, I'd be headed to the bathroom to freshen up.

"What the hells' goin' on in there, Black?" Max asked

through the connector. *"Haven't heard from you. Graham and Fay are back. My bandages are gone and it ain't gettin' any warmer out here. Tick-tock, rookie."*

"Not now," I hissed as I smiled sweetly at the old lady.

"Never seen you here before," she said.

"I heard about it from a friend."

"Yeah? Who would that be?"

"Baudelaire."

She shook her head and turned her lips down to show that she was impressed. "Baudelaire is a good friend to have."

"You seen him around?"

She was two moves away from beating me, but she moved a pawn. It was a throwaway move.

"Just recently, actually," she answered.

"What's your name?" I asked, looking over my shoulder to see if there was anyone whose look fit the name of Baudelaire.

I turned back to see her grinning.

Not good.

"Baudelaire, Miss Black," she said as all the wizards in the place stood up and faced me. "She looks a lot like me."

Trap.

"Uh, Max...help?" I said as I transformed into a tiger.

CHAPTER 41

The shit hit the fan.

Endofyer came flying into the room the instant I'd called for help. He was followed by Max, Bob, Lou, Graham, and Fay. Wizards were flinging imbued items left and right, causing all sorts of havoc as they did their best to battle against my fellow officers.

"You really should have gotten out of your chair before changing, Miss Black," Baudelaire laughed as she casually got up from the table and backed away toward a side door.

She flicked her wrist and a mass of heat blasted through my body, dragging a wail from my core that silenced the battle for a moment.

"What are you looking at?" Baudelaire hollered from her position at the exit. "Kill them!"

The pain subsided, leaving me on the brink of exhaustion.

I didn't feel so good. Baudelaire had cast a spell on me. But what was it?

The wizard gave me one last smile. "It was nice to have met you, Miss Black. Too bad it will have to be the last time."

With that, she left the building and there wasn't a damn thing I could do about it.

"Holy shit!" Bob shouted as he dropped one of the wizards near him.

He approached me as if I had a bomb strapped to me.

"What's your problem?" I asked, my strength slowly returning.

"Bethany…" Bob started to say.

Then it hit me.

Did I just speak out loud?

"Bob?" I asked, adrenaline pouring in. "Bob, what's going on?"

I looked down at my front paws and then back at my tail. Everything looked normal. But why was I speaking with my own voice? Why weren't the words coming out as growls?

"Uh, listen, Bethany, do me a favor and don't change back. We gotta have you checked out."

I swallowed hard. "Tell me what you see, Bob."

"I see you."

"You see me?" I felt my eye twitching. "What the hell does that mean, Bob? Obviously you see me!"

"Sorry, sorry," he said, holding his hands out as a wizard flew past, courtesy of Lou. "I see your face on your tiger body."

"HO! SHIT!" Lou screamed as he slid to a halt in front of us. "What the hell, BB?"

"A wizard cast a spell on me. Where's Max?"

As if on cue, Max said, *"Backup is here. Where the hell are you, Black? We have to find the entrance to the basement."*

"She's been hit with a spell," Bob answered for me.

"Wait," I said to Bob. "When did you get keyed into the connector?"

"We're deputies now, BB!"

"Where was she hit?" Max asked.

"Her whole body," Lou said, his face still registering shock.

"I mean where the hell are you, morons!"

"The chess club ain't that big," Bob replied.

"Yeah, moron," Lou stated.

Bob and Lou had both crossed their arms, looked at each other, and gave a quick, firm nod.

It was always better for them to have a common enemy.

"Near the side exit," I answered. *"Baudelaire got away."*

"For fuck's sake, Black," Max moaned. I could see him flying our way. *"Maybe you're just not cut out for this line of work. I mean, you can't seem to keep anyone in..."* His mouth dropped open as he blurted aloud, "Holy shit bananas! What happened to you?"

"Baudelaire," I answered with a dark look.

"Okay," he said, looking disgusted. "*This* time you have a valid excuse."

"Promise me you won't change back," Bob repeated, clearly ignoring the discussion between me and Max.

"No," I replied.

"Seriously, BB," he rasped. "If you do, there's no telling what will happen."

"Yeah," agreed Lou, "you could end up as a woman with a tiger face."

"Which could be cool," Bob noted.

"It wouldn't be cool, Bob," Lou argued. "It would be disturbing. And maybe even permanent!"

"Yeah, yeah, I'm just sayin'."

"I'm sorry to interrupt this riveting discourse," Sir Pickle said through the connector, *"but there happens to be a creature of immense power down here and I could use a little assistance."*

Only Sir Pickle could be in the middle of a life or death struggle and sound so reserved.

"We're in the chess club," Max said. *"How do we get to you?"*

"There is a door just inside the kitchen," he replied calmly. *"It's on the right."*

"On our way," Max replied. *"Graham and Fay, you guys stay up here and handle this mess, got it?"*

"Got it," answered Graham in a voice that was filled with pride.

The door led to a steel spiral staircase leading down. It was pitch black.

I stared ahead and realized I couldn't see in the dark. I sniffed at the air, too. Nothing. My tiger senses were dialed back.

That was not going to be easy to get used to.

I did my best to maneuver my paws down the steep steps. Bob and Lou followed close behind, with Max taking up the rear. They shined their flashlights into the darkness.

The small room at the bottom had a single steel door. Bob shoved it open and we were hit with the distinct smell of the subway. The New York subways have a sour odor that's hard to explain. Imagine a hundred plus years of garbage and B.O. covered with an acidic, industrial strength soap. Yeah, it's bad. Not as bad as the NJ Transit tunnels, but close.

"Set Almighty," Bob said, waving his hands in front of his face.

Goblin noses were almost as sensitive as a tiger's.

"We're down here, Sir Pickle," I informed him.

"Do you see the double doors at the end of the hallway?"

"Yes."

"I'm in there."

CHAPTER 42

It was a nasty sight.

Sir Pickle and Jonny, now a goblin-weretiger amalgamite were squaring off like a couple of fighters in the UFC.

The blows were strong enough to take most people's heads off. Honestly, I wasn't sure how the two of them were still standing.

"Again," Sir Pickle said, almost casually, "a little assistance would be most welcomed." He then blinked at me and said through the connector, *"I see that the wizards have done a bit of hocus pocus upon you, Bethany Black."*

Bob and Lou jumped into the fray instantly and managed to knock Jonny to the ground, but they were launched into the air by the goblin, who then jumped right back into it with Sir Pickle.

I had a thousand questions but they'd have to wait.

Max pulled out his gun and started pointing it at the mass of bodies, obviously waiting for a good shot.

Something in me panicked.

I jumped into the mess, cannoning into Jonny and tackling him to the ground. I tried to pin him, but his strength was too much for me.

He rolled away and stood facing us, panting hard.

Blood flowed from his mouth and he stumbled forward. I made a move to help him but he roared at me in that high-pitched voice.

I felt awful for the poor guy.

Sure, he was a mob soldier, but from what I could tell, most goblins in New York were sucked into the mob by default.

I transformed back to my human form and felt like shit in an instant. I managed to stay upright, but just barely.

Bob, Lou, and Max all guffawed at the same moment.

"What are you looking at?" I asked.

"Some fucked up shit," Bob breathed.

"You said it, cuz," agreed Lou.

"That is indeed mighty intercoursed," Sir Pickle chimed.

I spun my head around but it felt like a bowling ball. "What are you talking about?"

"You ever heard of bedhead, Black?" Max asked. "You got tiger head." He then held up a finger. "As a side note, seein' a tiger speak English is seriously fucked up."

I looked from face to face, all of them nodding in agreement with Max.

I didn't have time to worry about it. I refocused on Jonny.

"You okay, Jonny?" I asked. "You in there?"

The creature blinked heavily, his tongue lolling out.

"Black, get out of the way!" Max yelled.

Yeah, I knew my partner was standing behind me, waiting for a clear shot, but I wasn't going to give it to him.

"There's a better way!" I yelled back.

"No! There isn't!"

"I'll handle him," I argued, "just find a way to take him down."

"Dammit, Black!" Max yelled.

I spun on him. "Listen to me, Max. Fay's mother is a wizard who knows about this stuff, remember?" He looked unsure. "If we kill him, we won't be able to learn anything about what the wizards have done."

Max's entire face twitched, but he slowly lowered the gun.

"What's your plan, then?" he rasped. "And it better be a good one, because Jonny's going to be back in full form any second now."

I nodded and turned toward Sir Pickle, trying to keep my voice calm for Jonny's sake. "Can you think of something? Something that won't hurt him?"

"What would you..." he started to say, before he realized he wasn't standing up straight. A large portion of his scalp was coming off, but he knew his manners, that guy. "What would you recommend, Bethany Black?"

"I don't know. A trap. Like a Have-A-Heart trap."

"A Have-A-Heart trap?" he repeated.

"You have got to be fucking kidding me," Max said.

"Yeah, like a trap that lures him in and then—"

"I understand, Bethany Black."

And, with that, he ran off, his long legs carrying him as fast as a deer down the long hallway on the other side of the double doors.

I held my hands out so he could see I wasn't armed.

"It's okay, Jonny, we got you covered. Just stay calm and we'll—"

"He's getting stronger, Black," Max warned. "I'm tellin' ya, we're past the point where we can help him. He's going to kill one of us if we don't take him out."

"Don't listen to the mean man, Jonny. His mother didn't love him and he's trying to stop smoking."

If Jonny was in there anywhere, he'd love that I was taunting Max.

"Max is right," Lou said. "He's just regrouping, BB. Please keep your distance."

"If he goes for you, all bets are off," Bob added.

"No," I hissed at my partner. "You will *not* kill him, do you fucking hear me, Max?"

To my surprise, Max backed off with his hands up.

"I said I would take care of him, and I *will* do just that." I then pointed at a corner. "You guys just let me handle it."

That's when Jonny jumped at me, mouth wide and claws extended.

I remember thinking, *An army of these guys? They'd scare the whole city into submission without a fight.*

The force of the blow mixed with the fear filling my body allowed me to jump into full tiger mode again. Either Baudelaire's spell had run its course or my frenzied state had eclipsed it. Either way, I was just happy to be able to fully transform again.

I wrapped my legs around him as best I could to contain his furious moves.

His claws managed to tear up one of my legs pretty good.

I rolled out of his grasp. He came at me again, slowing down to take a sniff of my blood on the floor.

He picked up speed and bent his head low. He wanted to ram me but I moved out of the way easily. He slid across the floor and turned to make another pass.

Sir Pickle appeared in the hallway with a coffin. It was a heavy aluminum thing but he was rolling it on wheels. The sound of his approach distracted Jonny. I took advantage of the moment and ran past him.

He snarled and pursued me. I could hear him about ten feet behind me.

"Sir Pickle," I called through the connector, *"is there a place that's more open than this?"*

"There is a small warehouse just through the doors here," he replied.

"Get in there and get that thing ready," I said as I bounced off one of the walls, leaving Jonny to cannon into it with a shriek. *"I'm going to bring him to you, so give me a little room to work!"*

Sir Pickle hesitated for a moment.

"Move it, Sauerkraut!" Max yelled.

The vampire made an annoyed face and exited through the doors, lifting the lid on the casket at the same time.

I burst through those doors a moment later and slid

across the floor, slamming into a mass of boxes that tumbled over me.

Jonny was on me an instant later, chomping down hard on my shoulder.

"I'm shooting him, Black," growled Max.

"You do and I'll kick your little pixie ass up and down the street so hard that you'll not sit for a week!"

"We gotta do something, BB," pleaded Bob.

"You are doing something," I called back as I threw Jonny off with all my might. *"You're staying the hell out of my way!"*

"Tranquilizers," Sir Pickle interrupted. *"I don't suppose any of you has one on your person?"*

"Just the standard issue for when we're taking down werewolves and..." Max started and then he gawked. *"Oh, right! Shit."*

He fumbled through his pouch as Jonny got back to his feet and growled at me.

It was go time.

"Get ready, Sir Pickle," I warned my friendly neighborhood vampire. *"I'm coming in hot!"*

I took off at a right angle to Sir Pickle and the casket, as Jonny chased after me. I leapt up and rebounded off a wall that was exposed over a bunch of boxes. Jonny, proving yet again that he didn't have *all* the attributes of a weretiger, smashed into the boxes, pulling their full weight down on his head.

That wouldn't hold him for long, though, so I sped toward Sir Pickle and his open casket.

I jumped inside, laid down, and began rubbing my fur all over the place. The blood from my wounds covered the nice white satin bedding.

Then I leapt over the vampire's head and just hoped that Sir Pickle's reflexes were fast enough.

Jonny landed in the coffin and was about to jump over Sir Pickle as well.

But he stopped. He sniffed the bloody bedding and even took a lick.

That's when Max shot him.

CHAPTER 43

I panted as we all looked down at the comatose body of Jonny. I'd decided to stay in weretiger mode since I tended to heal faster that way.

Jonny's breathing was so shallow that he looked dead. It didn't help that his eyes were wide open, giving that 50,000 foot stare that screamed corpse. The PPD tranquilizers clearly packed one hell of a punch.

I couldn't help but feel bad for Jonny. Again, I knew what he was in the mob, but I'm sure Bob and Lou were once in similar situations and I loved both of them…most of the time, anyway.

Still, what had happened to Jonny wasn't right, and it was all because of my species' claws.

I wondered what kind of karmic price I'd have to pay for that.

That's when I caught the scent of oil.

I spun my head casually around, trying to act like I was just getting the kinks out of my neck.

That's when I saw him.

The Hunter was crouched on one of the rafters, near the back of the small warehouse. He was staring intently at the body of Jonny.

"Guys," I said as I continued my charade of stretching, *"I'm about to tell you something and I want you to play it cool. No looking, no freaking out, nothing. Got it?"*

"What is it, Black?" Max asked, sounding calm for once.

"The Hunter is standing in the back of the warehouse, studying things here."

"I thought he was dead," Max hissed. *"No, fuck that. He* was *dead."*

"Well, he has a twin, then," I noted. *"I think Jonny is his target, so we need to make this look good or he's going to launch a knife and make sure that Jonny is toast."*

As if being handed a script, Lou did a fist pump and yelled out, "We got the bastard, Bob!"

Bob winked and added, "And they called us a couple of washed-up has-beens, eh Lou?"

The gave each other high-fives, which only served to show how old they actually were.

"It's not like I didn't have a hand in things here," Max blurted. "I was the one who shot the bastard!"

"Yeah, yeah, yeah," Bob snarked.

"Ladies and gentlemen," Lou bellowed, one hand on his chest, the other motioning toward Max, "I present to you, Max Shakespeare, credit hog!"

Bob busted out laughing, slapping his knee and everything.

"Close the casket, Sir Pickle," I said as I fake laughed, which admittedly sounded funny in my current form.

The moment the casket was closed, The Hunter

drifted back into the shadows. The scent of oil dissipated, but I gave it another couple of minutes before saying the coast was clear.

"All right, you two idiots," Max yelled as Bob and Lou continued their tirade against him, "Black said the coast is clear already!"

They quit ribbing him, aloud anyway.

Max grunted at them and then turned back to me. "I don't like knowing that there's more than one Hunter."

I turned back into my human form and let out a long breath.

"Me either," I agreed, giving a quick glance toward Sir Pickle. "It definitely puts a wrinkle in things."

"There's the understatement of the year," Max said. "I wonder if he'll get paid for the kill?"

I nodded. "Probably."

"Oh, he'll get paid, all right," Lou said.

"Yeah," chuckled Bob. "Nobody's stupid enough to stiff that guy."

I was beyond beat. Fighting against Jonny was like battling an army. It gave me a taste of what others must have felt like when they went one-on-one with me.

"Good job," Max said, moving in close so the other guys wouldn't hear. "You're a tree huggin', vegetarian, leather jacket wearin' hippie, but you did good, Black."

"Faux leather," I said, flipping the material between my bloody fingers.

"Douché," he said.

"I think you mean, touché."

"I think I know what I mean." Max smirked and sat

down next to me. "Here's what we do know, rookie. First, Baudelaire got away."

I wasn't about to apologize again. "You think she's mob boss caliber?"

"Hard to say," he replied, rubbing his chin. "I guess we'll find out at some point."

"If she is, it would explain why the Hunter didn't kill her."

Max pointed at me. "True. Or maybe his only target here was Jonny."

"Douché," I said with a grin. Then, I nodded toward the casket as Sir Pickle began fastening it down. "One thing's for sure, they got the Blood Claw ritual to work better this time."

"Yeah," he said. "Translation: we still don't know much."

"Nope," I sighed.

"Officer Shakespeare," Graham called through the connector, *"everything is under control here, sir."*

"I'm starting to like that kid," Max said to me. He then fluttered up and away. *"Good job. All dead or..."*

I shut off the wide connection and went direct to Sir Pickle.

"We need to get him to Fay's mother's place," I said.

The vampire merely nodded in response.

"After we're done there, I'm going to want to talk you."

His eyes met mine.

He nodded again.

CHAPTER 44

"Every time I get away, they pull me back in," Fay complained as we pulled the van up to her family home.

Swanky place.

The five story brownstone building was just up the street from Lincoln Center on 66th Street and Central Park West. The American flag hung from one side of the lobby door and a flag I'd never seen before hung from the other side.

The doc took a look at Jonny back at HQ while he was knocked out. He was stable, but his vitals were weak. The doc argued for keeping him there, but she was overruled by Sarge.

We'd secured Jonny in an aluminum chamber, with a glass top. His vitals were displayed on a screen on the side. The top was glass, giving us a good visual of how he was doing.

I expected to tell the doorman the apartment we wanted to ring up, but once he saw Fay he smiled and opened the door to let us in. His grin fell apart when he saw Jonny's glass-topped prison cell roll by.

Max, Bob, and Lou all whistled at the same time. They scanned the place like they were searching for loot to poach.

"Is that a Caravaggio?" Bob asked, his voice shaking like a little boy's.

I watched, stunned, as Lou followed his cousin to the painting and said, "It can't be. The chiaroscuro is intense enough, though."

"Yeah, look at dem brushstrokes. No sign of sketch work underneath."

Max's face would have made me laugh, if I hadn't been equally stunned by the conversation they were having.

"Michelangelo Merisi da Caravaggio," a woman's voice flittered down from above.

She was dressed for bed, but she looked ready for a night on the town. Her long robe was adorned with stunning patterns and Chinese characters. Her lovely face's smile made everyone in the room stand still.

It was at that moment that I realized the whole brownstone was the family home, not just a single apartment or floor.

"Hello mother," Fay said.

She waited for her mother to reach the bottom step and then gave her a quick hug.

"Merigi," Lou said.

"Excuse me?" Fay's mother asked.

"We, my cousin and I, prefer to call him Michelangelo Merigi da Caravaggio, not Merisi."

"That is debatable."

"Not where we come from." Lou was being unusually impolite. Meanwhile, his commonly impolite cousin was staring at Fay's mother as if she'd descended from heaven above. His firm, erect nose was turning red at the tip.

"BOB!" Bob yelled. No one had asked him his name. "And you are?"

"My name is Cassandra, Bob."

"That is a beautiful name, Cassandra." He was wringing his hands when he awkwardly repeated, "I'm Bob."

"Thank you for seeing us, Mrs. Franklin," Max said.

"My daughter's friends call me Cassandra, Max Shakespeare."

"You know him?" Bob asked.

"Everyone knows Max Shakespeare."

"They're not my friends, mother. They're my teammates." She realized what she'd said and quickly added, "I mean, friends, too, but… Mother, please."

"I know, I know, borders. I haven't forgotten our last conversation. Nor will anyone on Central Park West from 60th to 100th Streets for that matter."

Cassandra sighed and walked up to Jonny's cell. Her feet were covered by her robe, which made it look like she was floating.

"Poor thing," she said. "Yes, I see the signs of the spell on his face and hands. But this…" She stopped and inspected something closely.

"This what?" I asked.

Everyone turned to face me. The sound of my voice surprised me, too. I'd been under a spell of sorts since walking through the front door.

"I've never seen the process so advanced," she finished while not taking her eyes off of me. "Are you Bethany?"

"Yes, ma'am." I realized I was supposed to call her Cassandra and almost corrected myself.

"I've heard all about you. I'm so, so sorry about the weretigers. If there was anything that could have been done, I'm sure our grandparents would have done it."

The weretigers had been almost completely wiped out in the Old War, mostly due to their own pride preventing them from asking for help. I appreciated the sentiment, but it did kind of come out of nowhere.

I nodded. It's the only thing I could think to do.

Cassandra seemed to remember why we were there. When she started to examine Jonny closer, I made eye contact with Fay who mouthed the words, "I am so sorry!"

I smiled and waved her off.

"He will stay with me," Cassandra announced. "I believe I can help him, but I make no promises. He's at an advanced stage, which is troubling on a couple of fronts."

"Why's that?" Max asked.

"Because, in this case, the more advanced the spell, the shorter a time it takes to perform."

"So yer sayin' that the spell will take less time to cast as it gets more powerful?"

She nodded.

"How long will the spell take to cast when they perfect it?"

"Start to finish? Five minutes. Jonny here was probably a two hour process."

Again, I got hit with guilt.

He was a test subject because of my species' very

existence. And if I'd only saved him from the mobgoblin's car before he'd disappeared...

"Black?" Max asked.

"Hm?"

"You gonna answer our hostess' question?"

"Sorry. What was it?"

"No, it's fine, Officer Shakespeare," Cassandra said. "I asked if you'd be willing to let me take some blood?"

"Sure," I answered, confused. "May I ask why?"

"It could have some healing effects on his current condition."

"I don't have much left after our last little adventure, but I'll give you what I have."

"Delightful," she said. She walked into a nearby room.

"Come on, people," Max said. "Let's let the nice lady do her thing. You too, Kitten Tails," he added to Bob and Lou.

Usually it was Bob who frowned at Max when he used that nickname for them. But Lou was already glaring at Cassandra, so he just shifted his ire over to Max. While Bob grinned.

They filed out one-by-one. I guided Bob by the shoulder and led him to the door.

"Here we go," Cassandra said. She pulled a needle from a plastic bag and slipped on a pair of rubber gloves. I rolled up my sleeve. The whole process took about 30 seconds. Cassandra smiled up at me as she pulled the needle out.

"Perfect," she said. "Thank you."

"I hope it helps."

"I do, too."

I rolled my sleeves back down.

"Bethany?" Cassandra asked.

"Yes?"

"I'd love to chat with you when you get the chance. Would you like to come for tea?"

"Uh, sure," I said. "Once things calm down a little bit."

She chuckled. "From what Fay has told me, that won't be anytime soon. Whenever you'd like, dear. I'm a bit of a scholar when it comes to weretigers. We can meet at Eduardo's, a cafe just down the street. It's lovely."

"That sounds fun. I'll be in touch."

"Wonderful."

The doorman opened the outside door for me and stepped aside with a bow.

I didn't like the idea of being a specimen, but I was used to it. Life at The Zoo taught me and Mike to tolerate the poking and prodding. As I walked back to the car I realized that I'd probably have to put up with it my whole life. There was no getting away from the curiosity.

Unless I locked myself in a room like Mike.

I shuddered, but not from the cold. This chill ran deeper than the wind.

CHAPTER 45

I knocked on the PPD lab's door. As usual, Pickle didn't respond, so I yanked the large door open and entered the darkness.

Pickle had used the connector to ask me to join him in his lair. On any other day, that would have been a welcome gesture.

But not this time.

I was angry with him. He was hiding secrets. If he knew there was more than one Hunter then he should have told us. My team and I were out there thinking one threat had been eliminated. That could have cost us everything.

I turned on my penlight and flashed it around.

Sir Pickle was brooding on a stool. He was a professional brooder from the looks of it. Kind of a cross between The Thinker and Van Gogh after he cut his own ear off.

"Hey," I called out.

He turned to me. I don't think he smiled, per se. But he did stop brooding.

"Bethany Black, hello."

"Hello."

"I'm...happy you came."

"Yeah, you look delighted." I was trying to joke around, but it came out as Asshole-ese.

"I was just thinking."

"Is there a lot to think about?"

"There is. This is why I have called on you to attend to my thoughts."

"Shoot."

"Shoot?" He reached into his jacket pocket and pulled out one of his custom pistols. The barrel seemed to go on forever.

"No, shoot, as in, ask what you want to ask me."

He harnessed the gun and turned his back on me.

"Max has probably told you about the coffin we used to trap Jonny."

"We only captured him two hours ago," I replied, "so I guess he hasn't gotten around to it yet."

"Oh. Well, that was one of my coffins."

"Really? I thought the whole coffin-sleeping-vampire thing was a myth."

"In some circles it is, but the Pickle family are traditionalists. I'm afraid I've carried the spirit of that intent with great focus. All-encompassing focus, some would say."

"Fuck 'em," I said.

His eyes went wide and he nodded.

"Anyway," I said after a moment, "why did you have a

coffin in that lab?"

"That is why I asked you here," he answered. "I want to share information with you Bethany Black."

"It's about time."

"I do not know why I trust you," he said, finally, "but you and I locked eyes in my lab and you did not blink. You did not speak. You did not move at all."

"I figured it was some kind of test," I admitted.

"You could call it that, I suppose. If you call a handshake a test."

"What do you mean?"

"Some mortals believe a firm handshake is a sign of strength, or connection," Sir Pickle explained. "Some do not give it a second thought and simply put their hands out to achieve the bare minimum required of them in that social scenario."

"So that was a greeting, then?"

"Yes, it was. It was an undead greeting that displays the calm of a soul. The focus of a soul. The…"

"The what, Sir Pickle?" I asked.

"The isolation of a soul," he whispered.

He was being honest with me. That still didn't help me forgive him for his secrecy.

"I'm glad the trust runs one way," I said.

'What do you mean?"

"What do you think I mean? How many Hunters are there?"

His eyes went wide and he bumbled for words for a second. "I…I don't know. I didn't know there was more than one. You must believe me."

"There has to be more than one. We both saw his

burnt corpse. He didn't just get up and walk away from that mess. What else do you know about The Hunter?"

I hadn't asked it calmly. I asked it in such a way as to make clear that our friendship was on the line here. He either stepped up and answered, or we were going to be nothing but coworkers from that point on. Seeing that I was the only person who hadn't treated him like shit, I had a feeling he'd cave.

Thankfully, he did.

"I now know that The Hunter used my blade technology to kill," Sir Pickle said with a sigh. "I also know that there is likely more than one. Or a copycat has picked up the mantle. But I swear that is all I know, Bethany Black."

"What about the underground lab? You knew all about that."

His shoulders slumped further. "Yes. I worked in the employ of the mobgoblins many years ago, Bethany Black. I was their top scientist. I built what they wanted me to build and in return they gave me the anonymity and isolation I yearned for." He looked almost sad in that moment. "That place was my main laboratory. It was also my home for many years. In those years, I created technology that humanity can only dream of. Much of it I did alone, but some I did with other great minds of their time. I also carved out dozens of hidden rooms where I could store my inventions."

"And your steel coffins."

"And my steel coffins," he affirmed.

We sat in silence for a minute. I felt my disappointment in him lift a little bit.

"Promise me you won't hold back information," I said.

He gave me that unblinking stare for about thirty seconds. "I promise, Bethany Black."

"Cross your heart, and hope to undie?" His eyes went wide. "Just kidding." I laughed as the tiniest smirk appeared on his face. "We're going to have to work on your sense of humor, Sir Pickle."

"If you wish," he said, bowing slightly.

I stood up and headed toward the door.

"I'm going to grab some Z's." I stopped and looked back. "Thank you for trusting me."

He glanced away uncomfortably. "You as well, Bethany Black."

"See you around, Sir Pickle."

"Good night."

CHAPTER 46

The PPD's Main Room was starting to get busy as I walked in.

The sun was peeking through the high windows above us, casting dusty streaks of light across the desks. Once again, I had to sleep during the day. It was getting to be a habit.

I walked into my dinky office/bedroom and was surprised to feel a sense of relief. The bed beckoned to me. Those cotton sheets and soft pillows were going to get used at long last.

I sat on the edge and took off my shoes, carefully removing the necklace my mother had given me, and draping it over the bedside lamp.

The sparkling pendant was a swirl, like a cyclone viewed from above.

"I feel like I'm in a tornado, Mom," I muttered. "Mike is in a bad place and I feel like I have to be the one to pull him out. I can't…I *don't* want to be the last weretiger, Mom. I don't think I could handle it."

I laid down flat on my back and sighed.

"Hunters, mobgoblins, wizards. I feel like there are only a few of us up against an entire army."

I rubbed my face, trying hard to clear my head. "At least I can take a nap."

"Rookie!" Max yelled over the connector, *"get yer ass in the briefing room! We've got a lead."*

"Or not."

I slipped my shoes back on and laced the necklace back around my neck.

I'd wanted to be a PPD officer my whole life, but being one was a different matter altogether.

"Living the dream, Mom," I whispered, as I tucked the necklace into my shirt and opened the door to face a new day. "Yep, a really messed up dream."

~

The End

~

Thanks for Reading

If you enjoyed this book, would you please leave a review at the site you purchased it from? It doesn't have to be a book report… just a line or two would be fantastic and it would really help us out!

John P. Logsdon

www.JohnPLogsdon.com

John was raised in the MD/VA/DC area. Growing up, John had a steady interest in writing stories, playing music, and tinkering with computers. He spent over 20 years working in the video games industry where he acted as designer, programmer, and producer on many online games. He's now a full-time comedy author focusing on urban fantasy, science fiction, fantasy, Arthurian, and GameLit. His books are racy, crazy, contain adult themes and language, are filled with innuendo, and are loaded with snark. His motto is that he writes stories for mature adults who harbor seriously immature thoughts.

Ben Zackheim

www.BenZackheim.com

Ben's storytelling adventures started as a Production Assistant on the set of the film, A River Runs Through It. After forgetting to bring the crew's walkie talkies, losing Robert Redford's jacket and asking Brad Pitt if he was related to Paul Newman (in front of Paul Newman) he decided that film production didn't "speak" to him. Since no one else on the set would speak to him either he knew he needed to find work that required minimal human contact. Writing fit the bill.

CRIMSON MYTH PRESS

Crimson Myth Press offers more books by this author as well as books from a few other hand-picked authors. From science fiction & fantasy to adventure & mystery, we bring the best stories for adults and kids alike.

www.CrimsonMyth.com

Made in the USA
Columbia, SC
28 May 2024

36274431R00164